"We're b___ ___row.

They'd been fighting it out for years in the courtroom. Emma defending the suspects Rick arrested, and him testifying for the prosecution and countering her at every possible turn. Battled all-out, without apology. But they'd always at least pretended that it was about the job.

Until tonight.

"You're going to make me think this is personal, Emma," Rick said. "That you're torturing me on purpose."

"Of course it's personal."

"Come on." He stroked the backs of his fingers across her cheek, then tangled them in her hair. "We've been driving each other crazy. Have been for years. And I've never been completely sure why. Maybe it's time to stop playing at this, and see what happens next?"

"Insanity," she whispered, tilting her head until her mouth found his. *"This is insanity."*

Dear Reader,

So…heroes and families? Can that really be the basis for an exciting love story? You betcha!

So many fans of *To Protect the Child* wanted to see more of bad-boy hero Rick Downing. Sure, he's a dashing police lieutenant. But there was such an edge there, beneath the surface, it made you wonder what was driving him.

Enter Emma Montgomery—a public defender who knows more about Rick's family's past than he does. And she's been holding a grudge toward them for a very long time. Which kinda makes the sparks and passion flying between these two a tad inconvenient.

Writing the ATLANTA HEROES series is a never-ending source of fun and discovery. As with all these exciting stories, *To Save a Family* brings you everyday heroes fighting for the innocents in their communities, and for the love they deserve in their own lives. Enjoy!

Oh, and keep a close eye on Emma's hunky firefighter brothers. Rumor has it they have a few exciting stories of their own to tell!

Sincerely,

Anna DeStefano

P.S. Please let me know what you think of ATLANTA HEROES at www.annawrites.com. And join the fun and fabulous giveaways at annadestefano.blogspot.com.

TO SAVE A FAMILY
Anna DeStefano

TORONTO • NEW YORK • LONDON
AMSTERDAM • PARIS • SYDNEY • HAMBURG
STOCKHOLM • ATHENS • TOKYO • MILAN • MADRID
PRAGUE • WARSAW • BUDAPEST • AUCKLAND

ISBN-13: 978-0-373-78257-4
ISBN-10:   0-373-78257-8

TO SAVE A FAMILY

ABOUT THE AUTHOR

Romantic Times BOOKreviews award-winning author Anna DeStefano volunteers in the fields of grief recovery and crisis care. The rewards of walking with people through life's difficulties are never-ending, as are the insights Anna has gained into what's most beautiful about the human spirit. She sees heroes everywhere she looks now. The number one life lesson she's learned? Figure out what someone truly needs, become the one thing no one else could be for that person and you'll be a hero, too!

Books by Anna DeStefano

HARLEQUIN SUPERROMANCE

*Atlanta Heroes

Don't miss any of our special offers. Write to us at the following address for information on our newest releases.

Harlequin Reader Service
U.S.: 3010 Walden Ave., P.O. Box 1325, Buffalo, NY 14269
Canadian: P.O. Box 609, Fort Erie, Ont. L2A 5X3

To my families—
the one I was born into;
the one God blessed me with through my husband;
and the one whose arms and love embrace me now
every morning of my life.

PROLOGUE

SLEEPING WITH THE ENEMY wasn't supposed to feel like being reborn, but Emma Montgomery was on fire in his arms.

"Damn, Monty." He groaned as her nails bit deeper into the muscles beneath his starched shirt. "I knew you'd be a tiger outside the courtroom, but if I'da thought—"

"Shut up." She sucked his lip between her teeth and tamped down the doubts for just a little longer. "Don't go ruining this by thinking, Downing."

Her warning made Rick grin, which had her stomach flip-flopping.

"Close the door. Someone could walk in here any minute," she whispered, inhaling a wave of aftershave that should be registered as a lethal weapon.

His fingers played their way up her ribs, until they were teasing the outer edges of her breasts. "It's after seven. We practically have the building to ourselves."

She'd been working late. Her nemesis had just happened to stop by her courthouse office. They'd bickered, as usual, then he hadn't edged away when she'd carried a folder to the filing cabinet. And she hadn't retreated, not even when he'd backed her up to her desk, his intentions clear. She hadn't moved, even when she'd realized that the sexual tension seething beneath their battles had never felt closer to the surface.

Rick had known what he was doing by challenging her. Somehow, he'd known she wouldn't retreat. Instead, her hands had smoothed up his uniform shirt to wrap around his neck, when she should have pushed him away and told him to go to hell. She'd even been the one to initiate the first kiss.

"My boss works late," she murmured against his lips now. She was also tugging at his collar and pulling him more tightly to her.

"Evidently, not tonight." Rick did some pressing of his own. First with his body, and then the strong hands lifting her bottom to the edge of her desk. He took his time trailing his fingers down her pin-striped skirt, until he'd braced his hands on either side of her hips. "Which makes you officially off the clock and out of excuses, counselor. How 'bout that?"

"How about this is a really bad idea?"

"It was bound to happen sooner or later," he reasoned.

"Later sounds a lot more sensible."

"You can go back to spitting venom at me tomorrow, Monty." He kissed her hard. "I know I'm going to regret this. But right now, you feel a whole lot better than being sensible."

They'd been fighting it out for years in the courtroom. Her, defending the suspects he arrested; him, testifying for the prosecution and countering her at every possible turn. Of course, they'd traded longer glances than necessary. Battled all out, without apology. Almost as if they looked forward to the weekly grudge matches that brought out the best—and the worst—in each other. But they'd always at least pretended that it was about the job.

Until tonight.

"We're *both* going to regret this tomorrow," she said. But she couldn't stop her hands from roaming over his chest. She couldn't silence her body's pleading for more.

"Kissing me like this, then threatening to put on the brakes…" He shook his head, his teasing was tinged with the kind of confusion she wasn't used to seeing in his eyes. "You're going to make me think this is personal, Emma. That you're torturing me on purpose."

"Of course it's personal." Did he really not know how much?

"Come on." He stroked the backs of his fingers across her cheek, then tangled them in her hair. "We're driving each other crazy. Have been for years. And I've never been completely sure why, Monty. Maybe it's time to stop playing at this, and see what happens next?"

The difference in their sizes had never been clearer. His strength should have felt threatening to her. His invasion of her personal space, as his hands held her head still so his lips could kiss along her hairline, should have felt confining. But what felt most dangerous and forbidden was the place deep inside her that wanted more of his touch, not less.

The part of her that wanted this man closer. Which was…

"Insanity," she whispered, tilting her head until her mouth found his again. Her eyes closed. Her lungs forgot how to breathe. "This is insanity…."

Rick began working the buttons on her silk blouse, swallowing each gasp she made. When she fumbled with the buckle of his gun belt, he groaned.

"Insanity it is," he said, as he pressed her back onto the folders and legal briefs scattered across her desk, and spread her blouse open.

CHAPTER ONE

"RICK DOWNING is a good guy, my ass," Emma Montgomery said to the gorgeous lawyer sitting across from her, while he munched his last bite of corned beef on rye. "The *good* lieutenant's at the top of my hit list this week."

Stephen wiped mustard from the corner of his mouth with a paper napkin

"This week?" His long draw of Georgia iced tea became a slurp, when the straw hit bottom. He lifted the glass for a refill from the waitress bustling by. "This running feud you have with Downing is starting to sound—"

"Personal?" Emma scowled at the waitress's departing back. Her own tea glass remained empty except for melting ice.

She gave her friend an expectant stare.

"Hey, don't hate the messenger." Stephen snatched their check and flipped open his wallet. "Downing doesn't exactly send me flowers after I've cross-examined him on the stand. But the last week or two, you've been on even more of a tear than usual. Is there something goin' on with this guy you wanna talk about?"

"He's been the arresting officer on every case I've tried in months. He trashes my defense plans, like testifying's a contact sport." And the man's father had been the enemy for close to half her life. "There's nothing else to talk about."

Exaggerate much? Stephen's raised eyebrow implied. He tossed two tens down as they rose to head back to work.

"Okay, so it hasn't been every case." She plucked a twenty from her purse and exchanged it for his bills. She handed him back a ten. "I pay my own way, remember?"

"No," her friend said, but he took the money.

How many years had they done the same dance? Stephen Creighton was a Southern gentleman, born and bred. And a gentleman took care of a lady's lunch. Even when the man was happily married, and the lady in question was resistant to all gestures smacking of her needing to be taken care of.

"It's just lunch." He grabbed their brief-cases and handed over hers.

"Right. And Downing is *just* another cop I have to grill on the stand this afternoon."

She hustled through the Courthouse Deli's double glass doors and into the atrium, fighting the memory of how good being in Downing's arms had felt. They'd driven each other crazy. And if it had just been about sex, maybe it would have ended there. But after the fog had cleared from her brain, she'd been horrified by her weakness for him. By how much more she'd needed.

Too much more.

She'd tried to pull away first. Tried to tell him to leave. But Rick had been holding her so close, as if she was something precious he knew he couldn't keep. And somehow she'd ended up clinging, just a little, when *he'd* silently handed her her clothes, put his own on and left.

They'd faced each other in court the next day, and practically every workday since. Both pretending what had happened was *no big deal*. But Emma had an entire afternoon of no big deal ahead of her, and her legendary control in the courtroom was starting to crumble.

She followed Stephen toward the marble stairs to the left of the courthouse entrance. The historic building was teeming with hustling bodies. Walking up the two flights of stairs would be light-years faster than waiting for one of the antiquated elevators.

"I'm sorry for being such a grouch," she said. "I don't know what's wrong with me."

"Maybe it's this case." Stephen turned right as they reached the third floor. "Your defendant's such a jerk, you half want the prosecution to win this time. And I think that pisses you off, as much as the potshots Rick takes at your defense strategy every time he testifies."

"Maybe," she agreed, even though she knew better. "I— Wait a minute. *Rick?*" They paused outside the courtroom where Stephen, one of the top independent legal-aid attorneys in town, had been representing his own client all week. "Since when is Lieutenant Downing, *Rick* to you?"

Stephen shrugged. "He and Kate's brother grab a beer once a week or so. Martin was already part of Neal's and my Thursday-night game, so when he mentioned bringing Rick along one night—"

"You and your boss are playing poker with that smug weasel!" Emma smiled sweetness at the strangers who stared as they passed by. She cleared her throat and toned down her rant. "You're playing cards with the police officer who lives to antagonize me."

"Rick's a good guy, Emma. Whatever hate-on you've got going for him—"

"Hate-on!"

Stephen held his hands up, pleading for mercy.

"He's just—" he started.

"Going to get back to court before I do." Emma smacked her friend on the arm in retaliation for defending the current bane to her existence. "Give Kate my love, you big traitor."

"You and Jessie still on for Sunday dinner?" Stephen asked as Emma headed for her own courtroom. "Luigi's, in Virginia Highlands?"

"Sure." She waved without turning back. "And you better believe you're buying this time. Remember, Jessie likes pepperoni supreme, extra toppings."

She marched toward her courtroom and her next showdown with the police lieutenant her job forced her to see nearly every day. The handsome devil whose dedication and passion for the law had gotten to her, even if he was the son of the man who'd helped ruin Emma's life.

Rick Downing is a good guy, my ass.

He was the enemy, no matter what Stephen or her hormones thought. And she'd damn well better not forget it.

EMMA MONTGOMERY had no business looking so flustered and feminine and flat-out stunning as she hustled into the courtroom. Rick tried not to notice the moisture misting across her peaches-and-cream complexion, compliments of the humid August day outside. Or how her blond hair curled around her face, framing delicate features and intelligent, cat-green eyes.

Good luck!

He'd run his hands through that hair. He'd held Emma's body close as they'd both lost their minds. Sure she'd shut him out after, and he'd secretly been grateful for the brush-off. But he'd sipped at all that skin that was as silky to the touch as it appeared to the eye. And now, his eyes were the only things allowed to feast on Emma. So he let his gaze drink its fill, while she ignored him so completely it was clear she knew he was there.

How the woman looked, he reminded himself, wasn't nearly as important as what she had up her designer sleeves that afternoon. Sitting at the back of the courtroom,

Rick forced his mind to focus on the job. Monty never missed a chance to work whatever legal angle she could. And their one-night indiscretion had only upped her motivation to bust his balls on the stand. If he wasn't on his toes today, one of the sleaziest criminals he'd ever collared might walk free.

She was late returning from lunch, and Emma was never carelessly late for anything. It didn't matter that Judge Mathers had been delayed, too. What *did* matter was that Rick was overdue for his afternoon shift and needed to return to the central precinct as soon as possible. Of course, Emma had been pushing all morning for one continuance and break after another, dragging things out intentionally.

Monty was as good as they came at her job. Her closing arguments could beguile a preacher into giving Satan a second chance at wings. But lately, even before they'd slept together, it had seemed as though her passion to defend her clients had turned into a personal vendetta against him.

Rick stood and closed in on the defendant's table, watching Emma pause beside the ex-con he'd arrested for possession with intent to distribute. Rick's irritation went from simmer to boil when Emma bent to speak with her client, and Tanner Simmons used the opportunity to leer down her blouse. Rick didn't stop moving until he was obstructing the creep's view.

"You're really okay with turning this guy back onto the streets, Monty?" he asked. The delicate muscles along Emma's neck tensed as she straightened. "I know you've got the ethics of what you PDs do rationalized to perfection. But this is a new low, even for you. I made a clean arrest. This guy's guilty as hell. You and everyone else here knows it."

Emma smiled her disarming, Southern-belle smile.

"Thank you, Lieutenant," she purred, "for making my point for me. It's because of things that *everyone* like you knows, that PDs like me fight for every suspect's right to a vigorous defense. Even the guilty ones."

Tanner's gaze shifted from roaming Emma's curves to staring Rick down.

"You heard the bitch," the gangbanger sneered. "Piss off."

"Watch your mouth!" Rick barked in unison with Emma.

Her scowl was all the thanks Rick got for helping defend her honor.

"I need to speak privately with my client," she said. "So, if you'll excuse us…"

Her glare promised Tanner it wasn't going to be a friendly chat.

She turned her back, dismissing Rick with an ease that she didn't quite pull off. Her almost-imperceptible cringe, as Simmons's stare continued cataloging her assets, said she wouldn't be heartbroken to see her current client rack up his third felony conviction in ten years.

"You're one ballsy bitch, *Ms.* Montgomery." Simmons lifted hands that had been cuffed in front of him. He rubbed the backs of his fingers along the sleeve of Montgomery's conservative jacket. "Just the kind of bitch I need by my side in a corrupt legal system."

Emma's composure disintegrated into disgust, but she eased away with dignity. Only then did Rick's hand relax around the handgun holstered to his hip.

Damn.

Get over yourself.

He'd seen Montgomery handle tougher customers than the piece of scum trying to rattle her now. And she clearly wouldn't appreciate any further intervention on his part. Still, Rick took a seat behind the defense's table, rather than the assistant district attorney's. Not that the *ballsy* PD would appreciate his concern, if she noticed him there. Which she pretended she didn't.

Instead, she stayed focused on the creep she'd been defending all week, staring Tanner down until the guy looked away. The bailiff announced the judge's return from lunch break. Emma sat, but only after edging her chair another inch away from her client's.

A.D.A. Shriver shot Rick a curious glance.

Rick was there to refute any bogus testimony Simmons fabricated on the stand. Which put him on the prosecution's dime. Still, he was sitting where he intended to stay for the rest of the afternoon session. For no good reason, really. Except that Montgomery was absently rubbing where Tanner had touched her, and the bastard was loving every minute of it.

"All rise…" the bailiff insisted in a booming voice.

The courtroom obliged. He droned on, recognizing the judge. Judge Mathers entered and sat, calling the court to order.

"Does the defense wish to call its next witness?" Mathers asked.

"Your Honor," Emma said in a controlled

voice as she stood, "the defense calls Tanner Simmons."

Tanner headed to the front of the courtroom, but not before his gaze tracked the way Emma's hands brushed down her skirt and across her hips. Of course she noticed the creep's leer. But she followed after her client, regardless, projecting business as usual to both judge and jury. And damn it if that grit didn't make Rick want the woman even more, despite how hard she fought every day to overturn the cases he and other cops risked their lives to bring to trial.

A scuffle at the front of the room, the bailiff's bark of surprise, jerked Rick's attention toward the witness box. He was on his feet and over the gallery's low railing before his brain could find the words—

"Watch out!" he yelled.

But it was too late.

Simmons shoved the bailiff to the ground, relieving the officer of his gun. His hands still cuffed, he pointed the automatic at Emma while he scanned the courtroom with wild eyes.

"Come here, pretty lady," he purred. His attention jerked to Rick. "No one else moves, or she's dead."

The bailiff lumbered to his feet, shook his head as if to clear his vision and stumbled toward Simmons, reaching for the Taser clipped to his belt.

"No!" Rick lurched toward the dazed man.

Simmons fired a shot into the bailiff's chest and reaimed the gun on Emma, never taking his gaze off Rick.

"Stay there, asshole!" Tanner insisted. Screams erupted throughout the courtroom. "Throw your gun to the ground. Everyone else, shut up!"

Rick did as he was told. In the ensuing silence, he lifted his hands and shook his head toward Emma in warning. She kept glancing between him and where the injured bailiff was sliding down the wall. Blood was spreading across the man's chest from a bullet wound too close to his heart. He made contact with the floor with a thud, his eyes still open, his expression empty.

Emma tensed to go to him.

"Don't move, Monty," Rick cautioned. "Play this cool."

"Listen to him, bitch." Simmons's grip tightened on the gun.

The bailiff's breath escaped as a death rattle. Renewed screams erupted from the stunned gallery. Pandemonium followed, wails of fear, people diving to the ground, running for the door.

Simmons shot into the ceiling. When that didn't get him the control he wanted, he shot toward the judge. Mathers toppled backward in his chair.

"You bastard." Rick took a threatening step closer.

"Don't!" Tanner snarled. He pointed the 9 mm Glock at Emma again. "I'm shooting my way out of this circus. And this hot little bitch is just the insurance I need to get me there."

His eyes were more than crazed, they were increasingly unfocused. He was high, damn it. Becoming more unpredictable by the second.

Screw playing things cool!

Simmons's gun arm shook.

"Look around you, man," Rick reasoned. "Look at the other bailiffs circling the courtroom."

"Shut up! They come anywhere near me, they even try to shoot me, and the PD's dead, just like the other two." More shaking, every muscle in the man's body now. His attention shifted from Emma to the two approaching court officers, both with their hands raised. Their weapons holstered.

"You've shot an officer of the court and a federal judge," Rick pressed. "Do you honestly think you're making it out of here alive?"

"I said shut up!" Simmons swung the gun toward Rick's chest.

"That's right," Rick encouraged. "I'm the one you're pissed at."

"Rick!"

"Be quiet, Monty." He nodded at the strung-out loser threatening to kill him. "Let your lawyer and the gallery go, Tanner, so we can work this out."

"No one's leaving here but me!"

"Is that right, you wasted prick?" Rick chuckled. "How are you going to manage that?"

Emma gasped. "Downing, stop antagonizing him."

"Be still, Monty." Rick knew he wouldn't be able to keep his hands off Simmons if the creep pointed the gun at her again.

He had to stay focused on the job.

"You think you can take TS down?" Simmons whined. "No way, man."

"TS, huh?" Rick edged imperceptibly

closer to Emma, even though that meant the gun's trajectory followed him. "What does that stand for? *Tough shit?*"

The bailiffs reached the front of the room unnoticed, their handguns drawn now. One headed soundlessly to check on the judge. The other circled closer to Simmons. Rick trusted him to take the asshole out as soon as he had an opening. The bailiff with the judge silently shook his head, then he followed in his buddy's wake.

"If you're so tough, where's your posse?" Rick insisted. "Why is a PD who can't stand the sight of you the only person on your side now? Where are your homeboys? I'll tell you where they are, *TS*. They're dividing up your territory. Taking your marks. Cashing in on all your hard work, while you're standing here surrounded by cops who're about to drop your ass once and for good."

"I said shut up!" Simmons shook the gun at Rick. Sweat flew off his arms, dripped down his face. "You're the one who's going to dro—"

"Now!" the bailiff behind Simmons shouted.

Rick launched toward Emma. He shoved her to the floor as both officers fired.

Simmons went down, shooting, too. He fired two bullets, three, before he was still.

Pain seared through Rick's shoulder, but he managed to brace his weight on his arms, sparing Emma from the bulk of it while his body covered her. The closest bailiff advanced, cleared Simmons's gun. He checked for a pulse.

"Dead," he said. Then he snarled something into Simmons's ear that Rick didn't catch.

Because all Rick could hear as he scrambled off Emma, knelt beside her, was the shallow rasp of her breathing. She'd landed hard on her back. He'd cradled her head as best he could. Tried to shield her after he'd antagonized Simmons into losing focus. It was a textbook technique—minimize possible targets, maximize available force.

Except…

Emma's hand hovered above the blood spilling from a bullet hole in her jacket, near her waist.

"Rick? What happened?" She reached for his shoulder but missed. Her arm flopped back to the floor. "You…" She coughed. Blood trickled from the corner of her mouth. "You've been shot…."

"I'm not the only one, Monty." He pressed his hand to the wound in her side. "I need paramedics over here!"

"What? Ah!" She curled toward him in pain.

"I'm sorry," he said, shaking as her blood flowed through his fingers.

"Downing?" Her next gasp was weaker.

"Lie still, Monty." Rick ran his free hand through her bangs. The silk of her hair was an insane reminder of the passion they'd shared, and for a moment he knew he'd give anything to be holding her again under any other circumstances. "It's going to be okay. You're going to be—"

"Tanner. Did he—"

"For God's sake, Emma, screw your client for once! He—"

"Did…" Her unfocused gaze locked with Rick's. She reached for his shoulder again. "Did he do this to you? What… What happened?"

"Shhh… I'm fine. Just lie still." Rick intertwined his fingers with hers. Fought down panic he hadn't felt in ten years on the force. "You're going to be okay."

She was bleeding out beneath him, shot, and she was worried about his shoulder. So, naturally, he'd yelled at her.

Calm the hell down and keep her alive!

"Jessie…" she mumbled, her eyes closing, slowly reopening. She clung to his hand, as if her life depended on him not letting go. "Tell Jessie…"

"What?" Rick searched wildly through the pandemonium surrounding them. "Who's Jessie—your guy?"

The idea of Emma maybe having a boyfriend, that Rick had no clue about her personal life whatsoever, suddenly hurt worse than the pain in his throbbing shoulder.

She shook her head, trying to speak, but she couldn't.

"Whatever you need to tell him, you can do it yourself at the hospital. Just hold on."

Wrinkles of pain and confusion formed above her eyebrows.

"No… Sunday…" When her eyes closed this time, they stayed that way. "Luigi's… Sunday…Jessie likes…pepperoni supreme… Ex…extra toppings… D-don't let Stephen forget…."

Where were the paramedics?

"Don't forget," Emma begged as her grasp loosened in his. "She… My daughter likes…" Her voice trailed off, her breathing becoming too shallow. Too fast.

Daughter?

Holy hell.

"Hang on, Monty." Rick squeezed her fingers. His other hand pressed against the mess the bullet had made of her left side.

Emma's expression registered no pain this time. She was out cold.

"Damn it! Someone help us over here!"

"TAKE A BREAK. I'll sit with her...."

"What the hell is she to you, man? Why..."

Emma's mind swam toward the voices she couldn't quite put faces to. The numbness of the dreams she already couldn't remember began to fade.

"Brothers will be back any minute..." That was Stephen, she realized. He sounded worried. Had she ever heard him worried before? "Make it quick, or there'll be Montgomery hell to pay...."

Her brothers were coming?

Who were they ganging up on now? They were always making a fuss about something...thinking she needed them looking after her now, when she'd done the looking after when they'd all still been kids.

A wimpy sound pierced the cloud she was floating on. Pain sliced a path up her side.

"Ah!" she cried again, realizing the sharp cries were coming from her.

"Monty?"

The second voice. It was closer now. He took her hand. Not Stephen. Not one of her brothers. But the touch was so familiar… So tempting….

Monty?

"You're going to be okay…" he said.

"D-Downing?" Her fingers squeezed. Clung to his.

Clung? To Rick?

She held on tighter instead of letting go. The way she had when they'd made love, and he'd bewitched her, mind and body. How could he keep making her need him? And why did her entire body hurt so much? Why couldn't she open her eyes?

From out of nowhere, flashbacks from the courtroom shoot-out attacked.

"Oh, God!"

The panic. The terror that she'd never see Jessie again. That her child would lose her mother too young, the same way Emma had.

Rick had been there, too. He'd tried to shield her from Tanner's bullets. Then he'd made sure she didn't give up after she was shot. He'd bickered with her. Told her to…

Hang on, Monty…

Her enemy….

"Thank… Thank you," she managed. Tears ran from the corners of her eyes. "For what you did. Thank— Ah! it hurts…."

"Then stop talking nonsense." Strong fingers brushed moisture from her cheek. Trembling fingers. "Stop thanking me for drawing you into that asshole's line of fire. Save your strength for something important, like getting out of here and beating me up in court again. I know how much you love that."

The genuine appreciation in his voice pulled a smile from her. Then the fear rushed back.

The courtroom!

Her client, undressing her with his eyes. Sneering. Grabbing the gun. Killing two men. Aiming for her. Firing…

"No! I can't…"

"Shh…" Downing insisted, from the darkness beyond her closed eyes. "It's okay… You're safe. Nothing bad's going to happen to you now…."

It's okay…

Her mother had said that, too, when Emma had been only seventeen. The last time all hell had broken loose around her. Emma hadn't believed in *okay* for herself since. Not really.

But she shushed anyway, just as Rick asked, her body slipping away from her. Her mind. The feel of his touch was the last thing she knew as she went back to floating.

Only this time, she was still awake. But not, somehow. Colder. But no longer feeling. No longer hurting. No more fear.

"Take care of yourself, Monty…" Downing said, just as he had when he'd walked out of her office the night they'd made love. "Get better, so you can go home to Jessie."

Jessie…

It was getting harder and harder to hear. She realized she was floating above them now, watching her own head roll to the side. Then the monitors hooked up to every part of her started screeching.

Rick jerked.

"Monty?" He patted her hand.

She couldn't feel it. Her eyes were still open, but she couldn't feel anything.

"Emma!" Stephen, whom she hadn't noticed standing on the other side of the bed, ran to the door, leaving her to look down at herself and Rick as the blipping sound that tracked her heart rate caught, hiccupped and beeped slower.

Fainter.

"Someone get the hell in here and help us!" Stephen yelled down the hall.

Finally realizing what was happening, she tried to panic. To fight. But she couldn't…

"Don't do this, Monty." Rick was still holding her hand, feeling for her pulse, his voice rougher. Harder. Like back at the courtroom. "You told me…message for your daughter. Jessie's downstairs…won't let her up until you're stabilized… Are you telling me you're too much of a quitter to fight for that, Emma? Come on! Fight for your daughter one more time."

Fight…

Her heart monitor squealed, flatlining. The sound bounced off the walls, through her mind….

Fight for her brothers.

Fight for Jessie.

For her clients.

But she was tired. So tired of fighting….

"Monty!"

A doctor and nurse rushed into the room. But the world was already fading to the kind of white where Emma could rest. At least that's what the seductively safe feelings flooding her promised.

They promised that if she let go, everything might really, finally, be okay....

CHAPTER TWO

Two months later

EMMA STRUGGLED through layers of disjointed dreams, back to reality. To the nagging of the doorbell that had woken her.

It chimed again. She dragged a pillow over her head. Whoever was out there would leave. Eventually. They always did. Two minutes passed. Five. Exhaustion insisted that she stay where she was. The bell heckled on. And on.

The simple act of rolling over ripped at her side. She pushed up, until she was sitting, panting from the effort. Swung her legs over the edge of the bed. This time her breath caught against both the pain and the mess around her. It was a little shocking, how completely a life could unravel in such a short amount of time.

Shadows peeked back, from every corner

of her bedroom. Clothes she'd been too tired to pick up or put away were strewn across the floor and dust-covered furniture. Drawn blinds kept late-autumn sunlight from encroaching too far into the gloom.

The doorbell rang again.

She squinted until the hands on her brass clock came into focus. Eleven o'clock! Who the hell was at her door at eleven in the morning? Jessie's bus wasn't due out front until two. Emma had set her alarm to sound off at a quarter to.

I hate taking the bus, Mom.

When are you going to be better enough to start driving me again?

Emma wasn't sure which attacked more frequently these days: her single-mom guilt, or the pain and stiffness the doctors said should have passed by now.

Knocking replaced the doorbell, punching holes in the fog that came with her meds. She grabbed a bottle of whatever was closest on the beside table, shook out a pain pill and swallowed it dry. Then she stumbled out of bed and made her way across the room. Each step was agonizingly slow, which wouldn't do once her fourteen-year-old sprinted across the front lawn. But whoever had dared to wake Emma up three hours early, could jolly well wait while she took her time.

She trudged toward the front of the house, wishing the demon at her door to oblivion. Her bedraggled reflection in the hall mirror didn't rate a second glance. She reached for the dead bolt and her side spasmed. Weakness replaced her anger, spreading outward from where the bullet had torn through her side. Desperation settled deep, to crawl back to her pillows and the oblivion of sleep.

But the pounding had to stop first.

She yanked the door open, not bothering with the peephole. Morning sun backlit her visitor. She squinted against the piercing glare. Long legs, broad shoulders, and familiar brown eyes were all her brain would register at first.

Then her world fell away, erotic memories and nightmarish flashbacks colliding. Her in her office, clinging to Rick Downing's strength. Both of them in the courtroom, his hand pressed to her side while her life bled away.

Suddenly the images of Rick swirled and mixed with the sound of Tanner's gun firing, the coppery smell of blood and pain.

Pleasure.

Pain.

Floating.

Falling...

"Careful." Rick caught her before she came close to hitting the floor.

"What are you doing here?" she demanded in a strangled voice.

"At the moment, looking for somewhere for you to sit down before you pass out at my feet. May I come in?" He stepped forward without waiting for her answer.

Her legs completely deserted her.

His grip firmed, and for a second she was grateful for it. Then she was mortified. Terrified by the flood of confusion that seeing him again brought back. Needing him—Rick Downing, of all people—the way she had at the courthouse, at the hospital, the way she wanted to lean into his strength even now, was unbearable.

"I'm late for a follow-up with my surgeon," she forced out. "This isn't a good time."

His gaze narrowed. "You were late for your appointment two hours ago. Since you have nowhere else to be, you might as well let me in."

She was too stunned by his familiarity with her schedule to protest when he pushed farther inside. The sound of the door shutting shattered her trance.

"Get…" She swallowed as she struggled for the words, the painkiller she'd taken challenging her concentrations, as well as her balance. "Get out."

He guided her down the hall instead.

"Let me go." She yanked her arm away.

Shards of pain radiated from the damage the bullet had done. She bit back a whimper. If it weren't for Downing, she'd have stumbled into the wall.

"You okay?" he asked.

She struggled harder to get away.

"Stop fighting me, Emma." He picked her up and carried her down the hall toward the den. "Let me get you to the couch."

He settled her on the cushions with a gentleness that felt too good. He brushed her hair back from her face, and the soft caress ripped through the last of her control.

Terror hammered through the Vicodin's protective veil.

"Get away from me!" She cringed against flashbacks of Simmons firing the gun. The bailiff going down. The judge. Then her…

"Not until I'm sure you're all right." Downing's face swam into focus, his expression a mask of worry.

His fingers drew warm, reassuring circles at her temple.

"Please…" she begged. It all roared back every time she looked at him. Her vulnerability. The fear and pain. She swiped at her eyes, her hand shaking so badly she missed. "Please, just go away."

He stood, then lowered his six-foot-plus frame into the love seat across the room. He studied her, looking more stunned by the second. And she could guess why. She'd lost weight. Too much of it. What did it matter what she looked like these days? She wasn't even sure when she'd bathed last. Washed her hair. And there Downing sat, as fresh and in-control as ever.

Ebony hair, resisting all attempts at style. Eyes, deep and dark like chocolate, the softest part of a face that looked as if it might have been chiseled from stone. Pronounced cheekbones, a high-bridged nose and as intimidating a jawline as she'd ever seen. Even out of uniform, everything about the man said, *hero*.

She slid the throw from the back of the couch and drew it over her lap.

"If you've seen enough," she said. "You can show yourself out."

"Not until we talk."

"What could we possibly have to talk about?"

His silence dared her to keep going down the *it didn't happen* track.

"It was just one night," she conceded. "It was insanity. We're at each other's throat's every day at work, and—"

"Not anymore, we're not. Not until you knock this off and get your butt back to the courthouse."

She stared. "It was just one night, Rick. It was just sex. And while I appreciated your help after the shooting, I can't imagine why you're here now."

"I wanted to see for myself how you're doing."

"*You* wanted to see… You actually expect me to believe you give a damn?"

Rick sat forward. "Why wouldn't I? Just because we've been sparring with each other in the courtroom, doesn't mean I can't care about your recovery."

"Sparring?"

"Granted, your animosity has always felt a little—"

"Animosity?"

"We both gave a damn for at least one night a few months ago," Rick continued. "And I was okay with pretending it didn't happen, until you'd worked through whatever you needed to, but—"

"With you? I don't need to work through anything with—"

"But then Tanner Simmons turned that gun on you—" memories stirred in Rick's troubled gaze "—and you were shot, because I didn't cover you fast enough. And after thinking you were going to die at the courthouse, I got to go through it all over again when you flatlined at the hospital. So, all in all, I don't find it nearly as strange as you do, that I give a *damn* how you're doing!"

And he did.

And just for a second, his concern dulled the burning in her side better than anything the doctors had given her had. But the terror that was never far away returned with lightning speed.

The mayhem in the courtroom. Rick protecting her. Her clinging to him. Blood and pain and fear everywhere…

An answering gunshot echoed through her mind. A bullet not from Tanner Simmons's gun, but from a nightmare she'd been running from for fifteen years.

"Stop…" she begged.

She couldn't make the memories stop. Gentle hands pulled hers from her ears.

"It's okay, Monty." Downing had knelt in front of the couch. "I didn't mean to upset you. Damn, Creighton's going to have my ass if he hears about this."

"Stephen?" Her head jerked up. "Stephen sent you to check up on me?"

"He told me to stay the hell away from you at first. Then he thought maybe I could help."

"He thought what?"

"He said you wouldn't see him, or your brothers or your doctors, and that you weren't strong enough to be hassled." Rick edged back. "I assured him that the Emma Montgomery I know didn't hide from people. You're stronger than that, right Monty?"

She stared silently while Rick settled onto the oversize ottoman she used for a coffee table.

"So maybe can we agree," he said, "since Stephen thought this was a good idea, that I care how you're doing? And then move on to why you're holed up here instead of getting on with your life."

Her snort pulled at her side. "You can take your care, Rick, and shove it up your—"

"Okay, so we'll fast-forward over the friendly chitchat. Let's talk work, then. You know, you busting my balls every chance you get while you defend your clients." He plucked Jessie's picture from the clutter covering a nearby table. "Or, how about your daughter? I assume she's worth getting out of bed for." His attention strayed to the tattered old nightgown she wore, then bounced away. "Or putting on real clothes for."

"That's it." Emma made it to her feet.

Swayed.

When he reached to steady her, she slapped at his hand, her entire body shaking from the effort. But she stayed upright on her own power. She was finally feeling something besides damaged and embarrassed about losing it in front him.

"What I'm wearing and how I take care of my daughter are none of your business," she forced out.

"Fair enough." He returned her picture to the table. "Work it is. What's your timeline for coming back?"

Her righteous indignation downshifted into caution. She melted back into the cushions.

"What are you really doing here, Downing?"

He'd paced to the bay window that had become her quiet retreat—when she actually made it out of bed.

"Maybe I'm trying to keep you from making the biggest mistake of your life."

"The only mistake I made was sleeping with you and letting you think you have any say in anything I do."

"Stephen says you're not doing what your doctors are advising. You're not exercising, not eating, not getting back into a familiar routine. That's why you aren't well enough to represent the clients you used to be so passionate about defending."

"Stephen says?" She took a steadying breath. Her friend had better start sleeping with one eye open. "My recovery is none of his business, either. I'm—"

"Look at this place." Downing's gaze drifted over the newspapers piled beside the coffee table. The dirty plate Jessie had eaten last night's frozen pizza on. "Are you telling me you enjoy living like this?"

"It's a laugh riot," she threw back at him.

"And you don't care about the clients you're abandoning because you can't pull yourself together?"

"Abandoning? Since when do my *sleazy* clients matter to you, except how arresting them scores you points with APD brass and the district attorney?"

Clients she'd built a career around defending, until one of them had turned on her. Now she couldn't face going back to her office at the courthouse, let alone returning to a courtroom.

"Actually, one of my recent arrests is why I'm here. How about a single mother of three? One a colleague of yours is about to let be ripped away from her family." Rick's grim expression settled into a frown. "Would helping her be enough incentive to pull your head out of your sexy ass and get you back downtown?"

RICK WATCHED as Emma fiddled with the blanket covering her. The passion that had sparked to life while she'd told him off was fading fast.

"Go away," she said in a weak voice. "Please, just go away."

"Why aren't you fighting to get back to work, Emma? You're medically cleared for half days. Your doctors think your pain and sleeping problems and the rest would improve if you got back on your feet and out of this house."

He waited for her reaction. Any reaction. But something on the carpet seemed to have stolen Emma's attention. She was staring at a spot near his feet, her arms wrapped around her, while she rocked almost imperceptibly from side to side.

Lost, had been Stephen's description of his friend.

Emma had gone somewhere Rick couldn't see. Then she flinched so hard, he jumped, too.

"No!" She shot to her feet and stood swaying until her legs gave out again.

"Take it easy." He kept her from sliding to the floor, then sat beside her on the couch. "It's okay."

"Don't! Stop saying that." Her halfhearted attempt to push him away again fizzled when her fingers curled into the collar of his shirt. "D-Downing…"

He resisted the impulse to insist she call him Rick. To insist they were on the same side this time—that they always had been. "I'll leave," he said instead.

"No!" she surprised him by saying. She

inched away, but she didn't let go. The look she shot him was full of hatred, tinged with desperation. "Just… Just give me a minute."

"Okay."

The day was getting more bizarre by the second. First, his thinking coming here could do anyone any good. Then, he hadn't been able to keep his hands off Emma since he'd walked through her door. Now she was clinging to him.

He cleared his throat.

"Just for the record, I don't think all your clients are sleazy. My respect for what your office does is growing by the day."

"Right." She finally let him go. "Since when?"

"I know I've given you a hard time." He didn't reach for her again, no matter how much he wanted to. "I take protecting the public personally. And I've always respected how much you do, too, even if I thought you were wrong most of the time."

Warmth crept into her pale cheeks. "I'm sorry I let things get personal between us. And for doubting your commitment to your job. I never should have… After what you did for me…" She looked to the shoulder one of Simmons's bullets had grazed. "You were shot trying to protect me. I'm sorry…" She shook her head, pressing her fingers to her right temple. "But I'm not feeling—"

"Does it really still hurt that badly?"

"It…" She took a shallow breath, no longer looking at him. "There's still pain, but…"

"The physical pain's not the worst of it, is it?" He understood more than he wanted to about the kind of hurt no doctor could really see or treat. "The fear and the memories are the real battle. But you can't let them win, Emma. Giving up's not like you."

"I'm not giving up!"

Rick didn't call her a liar.

The dusty disarray around them took care of that.

"I'm doing the best I can." Emma made it to her feet and trailed a hand down the nightgown he was doing his damnedest not to fixate on.

He'd seen every curve and shadow hidden beneath it. He knew the woman's skin was softer than any silk could be.

"Taking care of my child is all I have energy for right now." Every word seemed to weigh her down more. "And I need to rest before Jessie comes home. So whatever case you're talking about, you'll have to speak with one of my colleagues if—"

"It's Olivia Sanchez," he pressed. "You remember the Sanchez case, don't you? It must have crossed your desk before the shooting. The woman's nine-year-old got busted for selling drugs at school. Then she was arrested for what we found in her apartment."

"I'm sorry, I… What?"

"You remember." He could see the connection flicker across her features.

"I'm sorry, I can't help you." He could almost feel her pulling further into herself. She weaved toward the front of the house, her hand braced on the wall, not once looking back as he followed. She got the heavy door open and leaned against it, panting, while she waited for him. "And I can't handle anyone being here, you most of all. Don't come back, Lieutenant Downing."

He didn't hide his disappointment. "No problem. I'll be too busy trying to fix the mistake I made arresting Mrs. Sanchez."

She hesitated, then asked. "Mistake?"

"There are rumblings on the street. There's more to this case than we thought at first. It's possible the mother's covering for one of her kids. And she's probably going to prison as a result, which means she'll lose them all. The D.A. wants a slam dunk with this one.

He's already playing it out in the press. No further investigation is planned. Not even your director is pushing for it."

"Why wouldn't Jeff push for someone to pursue your new lead?" Emma asked.

"Because the defendant's flat out confessed. And no one, including the Chief of Police, sees my source's information as credible enough to challenge that. Which means my professional ass is grass, if I keep making noise. Meanwhile, Sanchez's arraignment is coming up, she's been in county lockup for two months, and her kids are in limbo with Family Services."

"If…if you have new information that would change a grand jury's decision, then you should—"

"Tell her public defender?" He stepped outside.

Emma was still the most beautiful, passionate woman he'd ever known, but she could barely walk. She could hardly talk without hyperventilating. She was struggling just to get out of bed and be some kind of mother for her kid. What the hell was he doing there?

But he couldn't stop himself from pushing one more time. And he found himself wondering if Emma might need something like this case to dig into, almost as much as Olivia Sanchez needed her help.

"I contacted the lawyer in your department who's defending Sanchez now. Brad Griffin. He said he'd try to look into it, but that his client wasn't interested in changing her plea. That was three weeks ago, and I've heard nothing. He won't even return my calls."

"Then maybe there really is nothing to the lead."

"Maybe. The brass sure hopes so. There's so much press coverage, the Chief's waving an early bid for detective in front of me, as a perk for keeping the streets safe from women like Sanchez—and for not making waves about keeping her in lockup."

"A promotion, as incentive to keep your nose out of the situation?" Something flashed in Emma's eyes, an echo of the fire he'd always admired. "How nice for you."

"I don't care about the promotion." His old man actually thought Rick was trying to trash it. "If I did, I wouldn't be here."

"But you're on the department's fast track. You're your father's son." She'd spat the word *father* at him. The shadows had returned to her eyes. "The job is all that matters to you. Why not take this chance and run with it? Why obsess about a two-month-old case no one else cares about?"

"Look." Rick had never understood her bitterness toward cops, him most of all. "Feel free to disrespect me or my father or any other cop on the force, if that helps get you fired up. But I care about justice, not just the job, and I don't think justice is being done here. And I've seen you go to bat for families like the Sanchezes. You never give up on families, Emma, no matter how low the odds of winning a case. Are you really willing to let this happen, if there's something you can do to stop it?"

She swallowed, hard.

"I don't want to talk about—"

"This is one of those cases," he insisted. He needed her talent at getting through to skittish clients. Someone had to talk sense into Olivia Sanchez, and he was the cop who'd locked the woman up. No way was she confiding in him. "This defendant and her boys need someone like you to fight for them. Don't hold the mess between us against this family. The system's no place for a kid who's lost both parents. Which is exactly where Olivia Sanchez's boys are going to wind up if she goes to prison for something she didn't do."

"I…" Emma's beautiful expression had never looked more confused. *Lost.* "I… I can't."

"I'll help you," he heard himself promise, when he'd come to tempt her to take the case on, so he could back the hell away. "Whatever you need to do the job for these people, I'll make sure you have it."

"If my office doesn't think there's anything worth pursuing…"

She swayed, fading before his eyes again.

He steadied her. He couldn't help himself. He might never get another chance to touch her. When she stiffened, he made himself let her go.

"Obviously—" her voice was almost unrecognizable "—I'm the last person who can help you with whatever battle you're fighting."

"That's too bad." Rick turned away, realizing he'd made things worse for both of them by coming. "You've never backed down from a challenge before, Monty. Certainly not when you had a chance to torch one of my collars. It's too bad you had to go and pick now to lose your nerve."

CHAPTER THREE

"Do YOU STILL AGREE with the district attorney's office, Lieutenant? Is Olivia Sanchez a danger to her own family, and to children all over Atlanta?"

If the bleached blond *Channel 27 News* reporter shoved the microphone any closer to Rick's face, Carter Downing thought, the broad was going to experience the business end of the damn thing in a particularly uncomfortable body cavity. His Rickie wasn't going to—

"Put up with crap like that!" Carter yelled at the television screen.

Then he downed another shot of bourbon.

"The Atlanta Police Department has no official position about the D.A.'s press release—" His boy recited from the same cheat sheet Carter had memorized decades ago. It was the kind of politically correct drivel cops were expected to use to keep the press off the department's back. "Except to support requests for further investigation into any open case."

The reporter flipped her bangs out of her face and did a neat sidestep, maintaining her profile for the hustling cameraman. All while keeping pace with Rick's long strides.

"But tomorrow's *Atlanta Herald* morning edition will include a quote of you saying that you believe you may have made a mistake when you arrested—"

"There is no quote." Rick pushed through the double doors that led beyond the Atlanta Police Department's receiving area, giving the press his back.

"But according to sources…" the woman continued as the doors whooshed shut, the two halves coming together in an Official Personnel Only sign that the camera zoomed in on.

"Well, there you have it," the reporter said into the lens. "This is Charlotte Billings, reporting *Live at Noon* from Atlanta Police Department's central precinct, for Channel 27's *Hot Lunch Zone*. No *official* denial of an unnamed source's claim that the police and both the D.A. and public defender's office are close to blows over the upcoming Olivia Sanchez drug indictment. Stay tuned for updates throughout the day, and a full recap at—"

"Damn leeches!" Carter clicked the remote off and flipped the silent TV the bird for good measure. "Can't let a man do his job without sensa…sensational…" The word he was trying to form rolled around on his tongue like a slippery marble he couldn't quite spit out. Another sip of his second highball that morning lubricated things nicely. "…without sensationalizzzing things just to score ratings…."

And he should know. A retired detective. A decorated officer with one of the department's highest arrest rates of his generation, Carter had seen more than one good career trashed by journalists just like the barracuda who'd been hounding his son. It took almost as much cunning and guile to juggle community perception of the job, as it did to actually keep career criminals and upstart wannabes off the street.

And his boy seemed to be playing into the leeches' hands these days.

Melissa had always known how to help keep Carter's temper under control, when the press had hounded a little too hard on one high-profile case after another. Carter had had his wife then, to soothe away the rough edges and keep his eye on the bigger picture.

But Rick… There was nobody but Carter to knock him upside the head, when he needed a refresher course on reality. No one like Melissa. Nothing but the job.

Carter looked around his silent, quiet home and pushed to his feet, heading for the den's fully stocked bar.

He hadn't had a clue, either, just how little the job and all the good he'd supposedly done the city would matter, once he'd buried Melissa and his reason for caring about any of it. Maybe his boy had it right, after all. Better not to care in the first place. Look where caring got a man.

Carter splashed more liquor into one of the lead crystal tumblers his Melissa had picked out when they'd had the room renovated a decade ago.

Only the best for your retirement party, Carter. You deserve only the best.

The bitterness that always came with his memories of his childhood sweetheart, his first and only love, burned his throat along with the bourbon. Top-shelf bourbon, because he deserved only *the best*.

So did his boy, not that Carter was in any shape to help him get it. Lately, Rick was turning stepping outside the lines into an art form—which was either going to earn the kid a shot at detective, or a permanent spot on the Chief's *not-promotable* list.

Last year's tangle with the FBI could have blown up in Rick's face, but somehow he'd come out smelling like a rose. Trouble kept bouncing off the boy, no matter how many career risks he took. Which would have been fine, if the risks had smelled more of ambition than self-destruction. And the last two months or so since the shooting… Even his Rickie might not be able to sidestep the heat for trying to piss away the Sanchez arrest in as public a way as possible.

The silent house screamed around Carter. Rick had been carrying the load around here for too damn long, and it was making him careless. And all Carter could do was dive to the bottom of a liquor bottle with record speed.

Not that the boy had wanted to hear it, the one time Carter had been sober enough to pass along his pearls of wisdom. Carter filled his wife's crystal to the brim and saluted his powerlessness. He'd failed as completely at helping his boy as he'd failed his Melissa.

"TELL ME I CAN CALL the *Atlanta Herald*'s editor-in-chief and demand a retraction,"

Captain Barrette sputtered at Rick as he slammed his office door. "And I'll consider not kicking your butt back down to beat cop!"

The man tossed a photocopy of the article the reporter had mentioned—faxed over from the *Herald*—onto his desk. Rick didn't need to read the details. Tomorrow morning's front-page headline was enough trouble all by itself.

Atlanta District Attorney 1—Sanchez 0. But Is the D.A. Shooting with Blanks???

"Sir—" he began.

"How the hell did a reporter from the *Herald* hear about your friendly visit to the PD's office before I did!" his friend and mentor demanded.

"I told you my suspicions before I spoke with the district attorney." *Weeks ago*, Rick left unsaid.

"And *I* told you to follow your instincts and work with the public defender assigned to the case. To see if there was merit in investigating Mrs. Sanchez's situation further, and try to get the woman to retract her confession. When none of that happened, I told you to drop it."

"Actually, you told me not to piss on the D.A. with this one. To make damn sure I was right and stop pushing until I had concrete proof."

"But you don't call making sure your gripe is the headline above the fold on tomorrow's front page pushing, is that it?" The captain headed for his coffeemaker. "You just had to go to the D.A.'s office and confront him directly, when you knew the story would leak."

"I barely made it through the office door, before I was shown the exit. Almost as if the district attorney knew I was coming."

"Lewis is a smart man." Leave it to Barrette to make something as simple as swallowing coffee look angry. "He's—"

"He's running for reelection. That's all this push for a quick indictment is about."

"No, this is about Olivia Sanchez being a menace to her kids and her entire community! Almost a million dollars of cocaine was found in her bedroom. You caught her youngest boy selling it at school, through a task force sting you were leading. And you had no problem with any of this, until a few weeks ago. Have any legitimate facts changed since then?"

"No. But the street noise is that there's a third player. I haven't nailed down who, yet, but it sounds like it's someone who—"

"*Someone* isn't good enough. The Sanchez boy's going to have his day in juvenile court. The mother has to face the music for the rest of the drugs. She's confessing, which saves everyone time and the taxpayer's money. The D.A.'s willing to ask the judge for the mandatory minimum in return, when he could push for a lot more. Sanchez is getting a steal—"

"Not if she's innocent and covering for someone else."

"If? The entire city is watching this play out, wanting a show of good faith from the department and the district attorney's office that we have some control over the drugs pouring in and out of this city. So unless you have something concrete to prove Olivia Sanchez isn't responsible for those drugs, or the defendant chooses to change her story, you're going to drop this. Now."

"I told you. I'm working on new leads—"

"That the D.A.'s office doesn't think are credible!" Coffee splashed over the rim of Barrette's mug. "Damn." He sucked his thumb into his mouth and shook his head at Rick. "Look, I know things are rough at home with your old man, and I sympathize. But—"

"Carter's got nothing to do with this."

"Well, he should, and maybe that's the problem. Your performance the last couple of years has you in line for the kind of early promotion any officer would kill for, and you're blowing it, getting obsessed over one case."

"I'm not obsessed." Not with a case, anyway. It was images of Emma Montgomery—stretched out like a goddess on her courthouse desk, stumbling down the hallway of her house, an empty shell of the woman who'd once driven him crazy—challenging him at every turn. He couldn't get the woman out of his mind. "I'm trying to do the right thing."

"Then get out of here, and keep your mouth shut about Olivia Sanchez, until you have more to bring me than secondhand street gossip. If you can't do that, then I'll have no choice. You'll be on administrative leave until you've worked through whatever's got you so distracted, you're willing to destroy your career over a collar everyone but you knows was righteous."

"That won't be necessary, sir," Rick said stiffly as he turned to go.

Time off? What the hell would he do with time off from the job? Except obsess even more about his alcoholic father, the Sanchez case *and* the sexy public defender he'd screwed things up with that morning. Which had probably been a blessing in disguise, because Barrette would really hit the roof if he knew Rick had tried to get Emma to work her magic from inside the PD's office.

"Hey, Rick…" Barrette called from his office doorway after Rick had already walked halfway across the bull pen to his desk.

"Sir?"

"You better damn well figure out what you want," the man said for the benefit of anyone within hearing distance. "A future on the force, or a one-way ticket to stalling out."

"BRAD, I DON'T CARE if he's skywriting his concerns over the capitol dome." Emma braced her weight against the kitchen counter, easing the strain on her body. It took care of the shaking muscles in her legs. Now what was she going to do about her voice? "You should be taking Lieutenant Downing's information seriously."

"Or maybe you should rest a little longer before you stress yourself into getting worse, Ms. Montgomery. We've got the office covered. This case is nothing. Don't worry—"

"My pretty little head about it?" she finished for him, resisting the urge to hide in the rumpled sheets and blankets and the shadowy bedroom waiting for her down the hall.

You've never backed down from a challenge before, Monty....

"I may be on medical leave," she insisted, "but I can still watch the news. Your *nothing* case is about to break wide-open in tomorrow's paper. Downing's second thoughts are already all over the Internet. Everything you do, or don't do, for the case is going to be scrutinized with a zoom lens from this point on."

Leaving an inexperienced Brad reeling, while the media hounded his every move. Which begged the question…

"Who's pushing you on this one?" she asked. "You wouldn't be slow-playing one of the district attorney's pet cases if you didn't have approval."

An assistant, just two years out of law school, wouldn't typically be litigating a case this high profile, period. Even with Brad's family connections and his drive to get ahead. And that meant someone pretty high up had decided Griffin's lack of experience was exactly what the Sanchez case needed. The long silence on the other end of the phone registered. As did the fact that Jessie's after-school pizza was about to finish baking.

Damn Rick Downing for making Emma care about any of this. But his suspicions, and hers, were gaining more substance by the second.

"E-mail me your notes on the case, okay?" she said.

"I've got it covered." He sounded determined, if not confident. "Really, you—"

"I'm your boss, Brad," she bluffed. Technically, she wasn't anything anymore, until she could rid herself of her meds and her ratty sleepwear. "So you don't have a choice, whether I'm there or not. Just send me the notes."

She was only helping, she reasoned. Her stock-in-trade was reading what others weren't saying, then digging until she knew enough to be able to help.

Like you read and helped Tanner Simmons, Obi-Wan!

She sighed at the nothing coming back to her over the phone line.

Sixty seconds till pizza, then she had to do the fully-functioning-mom thing. At least the pretending-to-still-be-a-fully-functioning-mom thing. Maybe then she could sleep for a while. At least the pretending-to-sleep thing, while her mind replayed every second of the shooting, her out-of-body experience at the hospital, and every touch she and Downing had shared, in a kaleidoscope of freaked-out images and sensations that made sleeping almost as much torture as the exhaustion of being awake.

"I'll scan your notes," she insisted. "Then zip you back any suggestions I have."

"I don't know…" Brad waffled.

"Exactly." The next time she saw Rick, she was going to kill the man for dragging her into this. "Let someone who *does* know advise you, just in case you've missed something. Better me, than the prosecution knocking a surprise down your throat at the arraignment. Unless you're already working under someone's supervision…"

"No, this one's all mine." Not that Brad sounded exactly thrilled by the opportunity. Bradley Nathaniel Griffin IV—the most competitive brownnoser who'd ever passed the Georgia bar, and he didn't want to name names? "And it's not that I don't appreciate your help, but—"

"You don't have to appreciate it." The oven timer's ding signaled the end of her patience. "Just do it. I'll look for an e-mail from you when I log back on later tonight."

She punched the connection off and slapped the portable to the countertop. Walking all the way across the kitchen to hang it up would be a waste of energy.

"Jess," she called as she bent to pull the pizza from the oven, lost in everything young Brad had said, and everything he hadn't. "Your dinner's ready— Whoa!"

She lost her balance, and the oven door seemed disinclined to move out of her way as she fell.

"Jess!"

Emma's left hand caught the edge of the counter, but her side didn't hold up under the strain. Pain jarred her, and her grip failed as footsteps drew closer.

Her right hand grabbed the edge of the open oven door out of reflex. More searing pain. "Shit!"

"Mom?" Her fourteen-year-old made it to the kitchen as Emma collapsed to the floor, cradling her burned palm to her chest. "Mom!"

Jessie took in the scene, slammed the oven door closed, grabbed the portable phone with one hand and scooped a handful of ice from the freezer with the other. She dropped to her knees and skidded to Emma's side, dialing already. All in a blur of seconds.

Emma could only stare as her *little girl* mothered the heck out of her.

Perfect!

"Here." Jessie pressed the ice to Emma's hand. "Uncle Randy!" she said into the receiver. "Mom's hurt herself, and—"

Emma yanked the phone away and jabbed the off button.

"Mom!"

"I'm fine." Emma drew her legs under her and pushed with her good hand.

Her daughter lent her shoulder to the cause. But after several rounds of starting, stalling when Emma's side caught, stopping for her to catch her breath and trying again, they collapsed back on the floor. Crying wasn't going to happen, so a weak giggle escaped Emma instead.

A lousy pizza. She couldn't even heat a lousy frozen pizza without falling on her face.

Jessie's answering laugh took the sting out of the moment's humiliation. The carefree sound was the kind of music Emma would take any way she could get it, even if it meant kissing linoleum every day. She was still rubbing her side when the doorbell rang.

Her brothers lived too damn close for comfort.

In a flash of jeans and trendy sneakers, Jessie was up and running for the front of the house.

"Jessie, don't!"

Damn it.

Emma struggled to stand, because she refused to be lying at her baby brother's feet as he galloped to the rescue. She tossed the melting ice toward the sink, while she pictured again the face of the man she'd like to take a swing at for the chaos he'd turned the last six hours of her life into.

Except suddenly it seemed like a better deal to face Downing instead of Randy.

And wanting Rick back, desperately wanting to feel his touch again, while he pushed her to butt into a case that was none of her business… That compulsion alone was proof that her bed and her meds were exactly what Emma needed.

She hadn't quite pulled together the bathrobe she'd thrown on over her nightgown, or her sanity, by the time a very large, very upset man appeared in her kitchen doorway.

CHAPTER FOUR

"I'M FINE." EMMA WIPED her dripping hands on her robe. "Everything's under control."

"Really?" Her firefighter brother scowled as he took in the scene.

On cue, the fire alarm began screeching bloody murder.

"The pizza!" Emma whirled to face the smoke billowing from the stove vent. And her body kept whirling, instead of stepping toward her daughter's scorched dinner the way she'd told it to.

Randy saved her from another up-close-and-personal with the floor, deposited her in a nearby chair, then tossed the charred pizza, pan and all, into the sink with her ice. The nearest kitchen towel became a passable fan. He waved it beneath the whining detector as Jessie slunk in, her hands protecting her ears from the alarm's sonic decibels.

"Traitor," Emma shouted over the mayhem.

Randy gave up quieting the alarm with the towel. He stretched his long arms, jumped the few inches he lacked, flipped the hinge so the casing would drop open, then deftly popped the batteries out with his next leap.

Now he was just showing off.

"Doesn't that fly in the face of some fire-fighter's code of ethics?" she snarked.

"I'll make sure it's working again before I leave." Which wasn't going to be anytime soon, his tone implied as he pulled her daughter into a bear hug.

The teenager stepped to Emma's side next, and hugged *her* so gently and carefully, the tears Emma had been holding in for hours rushed back. They streamed down her face as she held her baby close.

The same thing happened every time she pushed herself to do more than sleep. The emotions and the fear swamped her, the way they had when Rick was there, and she ended up making a mess of everything. At the moment, she couldn't even handle the working end of an oven.

By this time last night, and too many nights before, her daughter had heated up her own crappy frozen food, while Emma hid in bed. Before the shooting, she and

Jessie had enjoyed making dinner together. Gossiping about their days while they ate. Maybe going for a walk, or if it was a weekend, hooking up with one of Emma's brother's for a movie night. Today focusing on another mother's problems and facing a brutally honest police lieutenant had kept Emma up long enough to at least try to cook for her child.

Jessie's body trembled against hers.

"I love you, Mom." Jessie stepped back, her expression too mature for her age. "But we need help. You're not getting any better. Most days, you don't even try anymore, and—"

"Jessie." Randy sat beside Emma. "Why don't you go do some homework. I'll throw another pizza in, okay?"

"But I already finished my—"

"Get a head start on tomorrow's studying, then?"

Jessie pouted at her uncle. Emma chickened out and counted the variegations in the hardwood under her feet. Her teenager sighed, kissed her cheek, then left the room.

If Emma had expected understanding or concern from her youngest brother—which she hadn't—the foot Randy was tapping nonstop near her chair would have been an early warning signal to brace for disappointment.

"You're a piece of work," he finally said, "you know that? Your daughter had to call me. Your fourteen-year-old daughter. What, it was better to let your house burn down, than to admit to family that you need help?"

"I was fine." Emma clenched her fists, wincing at the added abuse to her stinging palm. "Jessie overreacted. I burned myself a little on the oven door, but I would have gotten the pizza out in time, if you hadn't barged in and distracted me."

Randy flipped her hand over. He got up and filled a towel with more ice, then pressed it to her palm and wrapped her fingers around it before sitting back down.

"You've lost your perspective, Em. And I think you've lost even more weight since the last time we barged our way in here."

We.

Our.

Her brothers were a crazy, safe place, where she'd always felt loved. And now she couldn't stand to see any of them. Because nowhere was safe. Not with them, or in the courtrooms she'd thrived in. Certainly not talking with the press, who'd hounded her for her story ever since her condition had stabilized at the hospital. Not even in her daughter's arms.

The long cubes of ice cracked in her grip as she fought to breathe.

"I miss you, Em, and I'm worried about you. We all are. You can't shut us out forever. You need help."

"I *needed* help." How did she tell them that having them there made her feel weaker. More desperate. More controlled by the nightmares and the memories, of the courthouse *and* of their mother. "But I've been out of the hospital for over a month, and I'm taking care of things fine now." She made it to her feet and dropped the soggy towel into his hand. "Clearly the five-alarm fire is under control, so thank you for checking up on me—again—but I don't need looking after."

"Em—"

"I need to get my daughter something for dinner." She shuffled toward the refrigerator.

"Are you sure I can't help?" Randy followed.

"I'm *sure*—" she slammed the freezer door "—that if you don't stop hovering, I'm going to scream!"

"Emma." His touch on her shoulder made her feel incredibly lonely, because she couldn't stand it. She inched away. "I'm... Chris and Charlie and I... We're just trying to h—"

"Help, I know." Except it was excruciating, impossible, to be the one they'd all relied on growing up, and now, she could barely help herself. "You're just making this harder, Randy."

But Rick hadn't, somehow. Not really. He'd pushed too hard to get her back into a courtroom, as if he had a right to expect anything from her, and she'd been exhausted when he'd left. But pissed, too, and stronger somehow. Until she thought about actually returning to work....

She flinched in Randy's grasp, as courthouse images flitted through her mind once more.

"Em?" His grip tightened. "Tell me what's going on, please. The doctors say you should be past all the physical complications by now. That it's—"

"All in my head?"

Her brother was the one who looked as if he felt helpless now.

"You think I don't know I'm completely losing it?" She laughed, then closed her eyes against more flashbacks. Let herself lean into Randy for just a second. "What is it with you guys today? I know I should be doing better and back to taking care of Jessie and my clients, and not being such a worry to everyone. But…"

But ever since the shooting, she couldn't stop seeing their mother with a gun in her hand, doing what she had to do, in the midst of her nightmares about Tanner Simmons.

"*Us guys* today?" her brother asked from what sounded like a long way away.

"What?" She looked up into green eyes the identical shade of her own. "Oh. Rick Downing was here," she blurted out before her better judgment could stop her.

Randy actually laughed. "Excuse me?"

She sighed, mentally slapping herself for opening the door to a conversation she didn't want to have. "He wanted me to help a defendant he thinks he might have made a mistake arresting, to—"

"So, the cop who got you shot—the one you've been legally dogging for years—stopped by for a friendly chat, when you can barely get out of bed? No wonder you're so shaky. What's going on with you two?"

"Nothing. It was about business, Randy."

The kind of business that used to help keep the past where it belonged—in the past.

"The man's got no business coming anywhere near you, if it's going to upset you this much."

"Relax. After today, I'm sure he won't make the same mistake again."

"Not after I have a little chat with him, he won't."

"Don't you dare," she warned. Rick had been brutally honest. Pushy. But he hadn't been unkind. And he hadn't coddled her ass. "Leave Downing be."

"He upset you." Randy clenched a fist so hard, his knuckles cracked. "You're sick, and he—"

"He didn't make me feel like an invalid! Unlike my family, he seems to think I'm capable of putting one foot in front of the other and fighting for something important. Maybe that's why it would be easier to have Rick here than you right now!"

"Rick?" Randy shook his head. "You've been obsessed with making him pay for years. No matter what any of us said, you couldn't let go of what his father did. Now you—"

"I showed him the door. And I plan to let Stephen have it the next time I talk to him, for putting the idea into Downing's head to come over here in the first place. Satisfied? He's gone, and you got to swoop in and save the day. Life is good."

She sounded bitchy, but she never talked about the past. Never looked back. Except now she couldn't stop the echo of the gunshots. Her mother's screams. Emma's own…

"Promise me you'll call if you need anything," Randy insisted as he popped the fire-alarm batteries back in and turned to go. "Don't make it Jessie's responsibility to take care of you, Emma. She shouldn't have to live every day being afraid of losing her mother. No child should."

Except all of them had, her and her brothers….

Emma couldn't remember exactly when Randy left. One minute he was reminding her of her worst nightmare come true—that she couldn't protect her daughter's beautiful spirit from the kind of fear that had nearly destroyed Emma when she was only a few years older. The next, she'd wilted against the fridge, finally alone, while her mind still raced.

About Randy and her other brothers, and Jessie and even Rick Downing. About the Sanchez family, and every horrible thing her own had been through. And the painkillers and sedatives on her bedside table. How they would get her out of this mess for a short while tonight. The same way they'd protected her for months, at least until the nightmares came back.

And the nightmares always came back….

"YOU'VE GOT TO BE the dumbest son of a bitch on the planet," Carter Downing groused. He dug his shovel into the dirt behind his Dunwoody home and popped another wilted tomato plant free, roots and all.

"And you've got to have the blackest thumb on the block," his son smart-assed back. "But that doesn't stop you from spreading the manure and killing the next batch of innocent seedlings."

"I'm a retired, Southern crank." Carter tossed the offending bush onto the growing pile he'd move to the mulch pit later. He dug under his next kill. "I'm supposed to do eccentric things I'm no good at. What else are the neighbors going to talk about? Might as well give 'em a good show."

"You're a retired detective." Rick took the shovel away. "You've been the talk of the neighborhood for the last twenty-five years. I think you can lay off the quirky, now. It's wearing a little thin."

There was pain beneath the kid's sass. And Carter knew he was more the cause of it than anything else.

"You're throwing your career away." He shouldered past his son, heading inside for the fresh bottle that was waiting for him in the den. Rick dogged him every step. "You're in line to take the detective's exam. You've made good contacts within the department, the local and federal agencies, and you helped neutralize that courthouse shooter. Two months ago, you were the media's darling. Even did a bit on the national news. Now this drug case is the perfect high-profile opportunity for them to screw you to the wall, and you seem determined to take the bait."

"I'm doing my job." Rick watched Carter grab a glass from the den's built-in bar, uncap the bourbon and pour.

"So far, you've ignored your captain's orders and helped every local news channel poke holes in the district attorney's pet case." Carter downed his shot and poured himself another. "Sounds like you're doing your damndest to torch your career."

"Of course that's what it sounds like to you. I'm stepping outside the lines again, instead of sticking to the rule book the Downing way. Right?"

Carter set the bottle down, then the glass.

"Right." He walked to the bay windows he'd added decades ago, so Melissa could look out at the garden she'd babied every day. She'd created the most beautiful yard in the neighborhood. In all of Atlanta.

His son sighed behind him.

"I have to follow my instincts, Dad."

"You sure that's all this is about?" Carter roused himself enough to say. The booze was taking the edge off the guilt, enough to face the truth. "You sure this isn't about that pretty public defender you were so messed up about not protecting? Or maybe getting back at your lush of an old man, who—"

"What?"

"The chances, the risks you're taking. They just don't add up. If you're trying to punish me for—"

"I may have made a mistake, that's all this is about. I'm fighting for a case, same as always. But this time, I may not be able to get it done by the book. Speaking of which, you wanna tell me why every time Emma Montgomery starts spouting off about cops screwing up doing their jobs, you seem to be right there with me, at the top of her list?"

"Who?" Carter headed back to the bar and sucked down another shot. "Emma who?"

The doorbell rang, followed immediately by the kind of angry fist pounding that an old man with a midafternoon hangover didn't need. Carter cursed and reached for his Jim Beam.

"I'll get it." Rick stomped away.

Away was good.

Enough with honesty and trying to make amends that weren't going to happen.

It was all good, Carter assured himself, happily forgetting about everything but carrying his glass and his bourbon back outside to Melissa's garden.

CHAPTER FIVE

"WHAT HAPPENED to taking it easy with her?" Stephen snarled as soon as Rick opened the door. "You were only going to talk to Emma about the Sanchez case for a few minutes. Maybe get her interested in calling her office. Then you were leaving her alone."

"What is this, dump on Rick day?" Rick would have selected a more colorful word than *dump*, but Stephen's wife was standing beside the lawyer, her knowing smile one of genuine concern. He motioned inside with his arm. "Come in, Kate, and bring your pit bull with you."

She was wearing happy yellow scrubs, and she smelled like shampoo and soap when she leaned in to kiss his cheek. Which meant she was on her way to the hospital tonight, instead of stopping by after a long shift on the pediatric floor.

"Hope you don't mind me tagging along."

She dropped her latest trendy purse onto the foyer table. "But when I heard Stephen arguing on the phone with Randy Montgomery, I figured this wasn't going to be the friendliest visit. Sounded like a woman's touch was in order."

"She's worried I'll deck you," Creighton said.

"*She's* already made a side bet on who'll deck who," Stephen's wife of less than a year corrected. "You two deserve each other, after ganging up on Emma that way."

"I didn't go near the woman," Stephen insisted. "I—"

"You're just as much to blame for upsetting her as Rick is. You're the one who told him how badly she's doing, but to try and talk her into weighing in on this drug case anyway."

Stephen didn't argue back. Mostly, Rick assumed, because he knew his wife was right.

"It was crazy of me to think I could keep from upsetting her somehow," Rick offered, cutting his friend some slack. "But—"

"But you *had* to see her?" Stephen asked.

"What did Randy want?" Rick asked his partner in crime.

"The guy's furious that you bothered Emma." Creighton held out a hand, and Kate walked over to him.

Rick rarely saw them together when they weren't touching each other in some way. His own fingers tingled from the memory of reaching for Emma. The softness of her. The firm muscles beneath that softness. Her sweet, breathy sighs, when he touched just the right place. The tentative way she'd reached for him again that morning, almost as if she was glad he was there....

"Why did Randy call you—" Rick clenched his fists against the memories "—if his problem's with me?"

"Seems my name came up when Emma told him about your little visit. You didn't happen to mention me, while you were over there, did you?"

Rick winced. "Sorry, man."

"He said she was pretty messed up when he got there tonight. The guy wants us both by the balls. But since he and Kate have volunteered for years together at the Midtown Shelter, he figured he'd give me the benefit of the doubt and a chance to explain."

"Nice of him." As petite as Emma was, each of her firefighter brothers was brawny enough to be a starting blocker for the UGA football team. "Great. Pissed-off brothers on my ass. That pretty much rounds out the week. He say anything else?"

"That I've lost my mind, encouraging you to upset his sister to the point that she almost burned her house down after you left!"

"What?"

"Her daughter's the one who called him, after Emma burned her hand in a fall and nearly set her oven on fire."

"She's fine," Kate added. "But she was upset, and—"

"What did you say to the woman?" Stephen asked.

"I tried to get her interested in the Sanchez case." Rick braced his hands on his hips. "Like you'd said when we talked, it sounded like the sort of situation that might spark her interest."

"And—"

"And she didn't exactly appreciate my being there."

"So you backed off?" Kate's tone said Rick needn't bother answer.

So he didn't.

"Damn, man," Stephen said. "How hard did you push?"

"You said you thought she was hiding out in that house," Rick reminded him. "And you're right. It…the place was depressing *me,* and I was only there for a few minutes."

It had resembled his father's bedroom the first months after his mother's death. Carter had barely gotten out of bed. He'd refused to open the curtains or allow anyone to let the light in for him. Since then, the man had made a damn shrine out of the back garden. Planting, then killing, plant after plant.

"I thought seeing you might shock her out of whatever's going on," Stephen admitted.

"You're a pair of meddling old men." Kate cuffed her husband on the shoulder. "Obviously, fighting to get back to work would be what she needed. Did either of you stop to think that maybe *work* is a big part of the problem?"

"Monty thrives on her job," Rick argued.

"Monty?" Kate smiled at that. Then she frowned. "Emma may have thrived on doing her thing in court before the shooting, but—"

"You agreed she should be recovered enough to be back at work by now," Stephen said.

"Physically, yes, from everything I've

heard about her injuries and her doctors' rec-
ommendations. But she's still weak, and—"

"Emma's as strong as they come." Stephen
shook his head. "She just needs to get—"

"Back on the horse." Rick finished for him.

Carter had said the same thing a long time
ago, when Rick had taken a bad fall learning
how to ride his first bike, and was too afraid
to try again. The same man who never left his
house now, except to plant the seedlings he
had delivered every week from the nursery
down the street. Now Carter was the one who
was hiding.

Rick had been living with the poster boy
for clinical depression. But he hadn't even
stopped to consider what the last two months
must have been like for Emma, no matter
how strong she'd always been.

"If she goes back to work, she'll have to
go back to the courthouse," he mumbled.
"Damn…"

"Ah," Kate said. "The light flickers dimly."

"I don't get it," Stephen said. "What
does—"

"I'll explain it in the car." Kate gave Rick
a quick hug, then looped her arm through
her husband's. "I'll be late for my shift if
we don't go."

Stephen let himself be led as far as the door before he turned back.

"I suggested you go to Emma's house today," he said, "because I thought maybe you two might have had something between you back before the shooting. You were always at each other's throats, but something had changed there for a while… And I thought, maybe…" He shook his head. "Clearly I was wrong. Stay away from her, Rick. Her brothers are at their wits' end trying to get through to her, and adding you to the mix is clearly a bad idea. Figure a way around your problems with this case on your own."

As if Rick wasn't already telling himself that.

Except, as he closed the door behind Kate and Stephen and looked back toward the den where his father always drank himself into a stupor, all he could think about was the lost, empty expression on Emma's face when she'd opened her door. Her hopelessness when he'd left. Every moment he'd spent with her in between.

She'd been trapped in her fears. Not just pissed at him, but terrified of reaching for his help, and blaming herself that she couldn't do more to take care of herself or anyone else. And damn it, he'd pushed her into feeling all of it even more.

He had to see her again. And not just because he needed her help with Olivia Sanchez.

It was time to accept that this morning had been about more. Rick had needed to feel her touch again, so badly he doubted he'd sleep tonight for still wanting it. And now he needed to be sure she was okay. Screw the case.

THERE WERE THREE GROWN MEN in Emma's front yard, and she'd spent the last twenty minutes scolding each of them as if they were still kids.

At least Jessie wasn't vegetating Saturday morning away surfing YouTube. And Emma's suburban neighbors hadn't had this much to gossip about in years. The spectacle her brothers were making would pretty much cover Emma's contribution to community morale for a good long time.

"Why are you mad at Uncle Randy and Uncle Charlie and Uncle Chris?" Jessie asked at her elbow.

"They're the ones stomping around acting mad, honey. Not me." Emma let her front window's sheers fall shut. "And don't act all innocent. You ratted me out to them again, didn't you?"

Her daughter did her impersonation of Emma's *give me a break* stare.

Emma retaliated by rolling her eyes like a teenager.

"Okay." She yanked the curtains back open in time to see a black truck pull to the curb behind her brothers' various vehicles. "Maybe I shouldn't be driving myself into town yet, but—"

"After nearly passing out yesterday afternoon? You think!"

"But if *you* think," Emma continued, "that I'm hitching a ride from one of the three musketeers out there, so they can keep track of every step I take and follow me into my office, giving me pointers on how to breathe, you're crazy. Your uncles' obsession with mothering me is getting old fast."

Actually, she was pissed at herself, not at her brothers. Pissed at the second thoughts swirling through her head, after she'd spent half the morning talking herself into doing this.

Jessie peeked around her shoulder.

"Wow. Get a load of that ass in those jeans!"

Another look out the window revealed

none other than Rick Downing stepping onto the curb.

"Perfect," Emma groaned.

And the hits just kept on coming.

"He's hot," her daughter offered.

You should see him in uniform. Or out of it.

"Who is he?" Jessie asked.

"Trouble." Emma let her *baby's* overdeveloped obsession with hot bodies pass, her mind too consumed with watching Rick approach her brothers.

"Is that the cop who guilted you into going into the office?" Jessie asked.

Damn Chris for not looking to see if his niece was around before letting that comment fly that morning.

"I haven't gone anywhere yet."

"You're up before noon and dressed…" Jessie gave Emma the once-over. "Well, sort of dressed. That's better than nothing."

Yeah. Emma had made it all the way to the kitchen in non-office-appropriate jeans and an ancient T-shirt before an image of being in a courtroom again had flashed.

And stopped her cold.

Then her brothers had shown up, Chris leading the charge this time, and announced that they weren't letting her head into town alone to check on the Sanchez case *in her condition*.

"Okay, maybe I need to change," she mumbled.

Actually, what her head and body were screaming for were her Vicodin, sitting on the bedside table she'd pass on her way to the closet.

Just a little while longer, she rationalized. She'd take them for just a little longer. Then she'd taper off them and the sedatives….

It was the same promise she'd been making herself for weeks.

She glanced at her daughter, who was still fixated on their lawn entertainment, and felt the guilt settle deeper. Their weekends used to be nonstop activity. Hiking up Stone Mountain early Saturday mornings, then having breakfast at their favorite bakery in the tiny village nearby. Shopping. Or Jessie hanging with friends, studying and working on projects and, most importantly, talking about boys, while Emma worked in the other room and made sure the girls had a constant supply of snacks.

Now her fourteen-year-old stayed in all weekend to babysit her mom.

"Looks like the Montgomery brothers

have someone else to be mad at now," Jessie said on a choked laugh. "How long do you think, before one of them belts that guy?"

"What?" Emma gaped over her daughter's shoulder, then stumbled toward the front door and yanked it open.

"Why can't you mind your own business and leave me the hell alone!"

Four male heads pivoted toward her, atop four sets of broad shoulders. For the first time, she'd realized that Rick Downing could most definitely hold his own against her hulking brothers. They'd squared off near Downing's truck, primed for mortal combat, her brothers ready to take Carter Downing's son apart.

"Go back inside, Em," Chris warned. Just two years younger than Emma, he was the only one of her brothers Rick might have crossed paths with, when they'd played on football teams for rival high schools.

"Why?" Emma asked. "So my *menfolk* can take care of my problems for me? Stop posing, all of you. Go find somewhere else to display your macho. My neighbors and I have seen enough."

Unlike the Downings, whose home was in the heart of Dunwoody, Emma and her brothers had always lived in less-elite suburban neighborhoods. But a Saturday-morning tag-team smackdown would be over the top even for Emma's neck of the woods.

Chris and Charlie looked torn. But Randy never backed down from a fight.

"Didn't you cause enough damage yesterday?" He advanced toward Rick. "Our sister doesn't need more stress, on top of—"

"On top of being talked about as if I'm not here?" she asked. Not that her brother noticed. "My hand's fine, Randy. Don't—"

"See, she's fine." Rick glanced to where Emma was leaning on the door frame for support. "Just like she's been *fine* every day of the last two months. Not that she doesn't still look like a stiff breeze would knock her down. But if you three think that's fine, who am I to argue?"

Emma's jaw dropped open.

She ran a hand down her jeans. They were obscenely baggy these days, but they were still her favorite. She'd thrown them on over the panty hose she'd struggled for ten minutes to get into. By then, she'd been beyond dragging on a suit. But jeans were better than wearing her robe and slippers to work, so she'd let herself feel a moment of accomplishment.

Of course, her stockings were already snagging on the brickwork beneath her shoeless feet. And she couldn't quite remember if she'd touched her hair. Or bothered with brushing her teeth….

"Keep your mouth shut about my sister," Randy snapped. "How she looks is none of your damn business. I don't care what you keep coming here for, you're not bothering Emma any—"

"Well, someone needs to be bothering her," Rick shot back. "Or haven't you boys noticed that she's terrified to leave her own home."

"Because you got her shot!" Charlie said.

"Hotdogging it in the courtroom," Chris chimed in.

Rick's hands curled into fists at his sides.

"Stop it!" She took tentative steps toward the idiots on her lawn.

Her feet shuffled. Her stockings ripped even more, feeding the fury raging inside her. Fury at all of them, and the fear and panic she could feel building with each step and memory of the shooting.

"Take it easy, Em." Randy turned, as though he was coming to help her.

"Stop coddling me!" she shouted, glancing

across the street in time to catch Mrs. Strumm pulling her curtains open an inch wider.

Once more for the cheap seats in the back.

"Stop talking about me like I'm five years old," she said in a calmer voice. "Or that I don't have the brains to throw you off my property."

"You heard the lady." Chris went nose to nose with Downing now, shoving Randy aside. He pressed a palm to Rick's chest. "Time for you to be on your way, Officer."

"Hands off," Rick warned.

Chris pushed instead.

In a flash, Rick had grabbed her brother's wrist, bent it at an obviously painful angle, and turned Chris until his back was to Rick's chest.

"Your bad manners aside," Rick growled in her brother's ear, "I came here for a friendly visit. And I'm not going anywhere until I'm damn good and ready."

"Stop it, all of you!" Emma demanded as Charlie and Randy burst into motion, each grabbing one of Downing's arms. "I want all of you out of here. Now!"

What she got instead was a front-row seat to the grudge match of the century.

Her two youngest brothers pulled Rick far enough away for Chris to turn and land a cheap gut punch. Rick grunted, but he brought his knees up and kicked. Chris, all two-hundred-plus pounds of him, landed hard and skidded several feet on the grass she'd just had resodded. Not sparing him a glance, Rick pulled free of Randy's hold and waited, patient and balanced on the balls of his feet, hands low, anticipating Randy or Charlie's next move.

"You bastard!" Chris snarled as he sprang to his feet.

"Stop it!" Emma shouted over the mayhem of four bodies colliding in a bone-pounding display.

She waded into the fray, noticing that Mrs. Strumm was now on the sidewalk in front of her house.

"Stop it!" Emma pushed and shoved and ducked until she could grab hold of the nearest bloodied shirt and shake. "Are you trying to get yourself killed?"

Both she and the man in her grip were panting for breath. His brown eyes warmed from anger to concern. So did his too-familiar touch. And that's when it registered that she was once more standing in Rick Downing's arms.

And it felt good. Comforting. It had to be

the scratches accenting the bruise on his cheek and his bloodied nose. His willingness to take on all three of her brothers, for whatever insane reason was driving him. She'd always been a sucker for the underdog. Or maybe she really, really needed her meds. Her pillows and her blankets. Her safe, hideaway place where the world and the past would leave her alone for a little while longer.

It had to be anything *but* actually needing Rick there.

Her brothers closed around them, circling like a threatening storm.

"Let her go," Charlie demanded.

Emma turned and blocked Rick from their anger, and vice versa.

"Enough." Her command came out more like a wheeze.

Dizzy didn't begin to describe the way the world was shimmering around her. Her ears were humming with a high-pitched warble she knew no one else heard. Rick's hand curled around her uninjured side, lending support as if he had been there at her back every day of her life.

Charlie's gaze tracked the gesture, his eyes narrowing to a killing rage.

"I said let her go."

"And *I* said," Emma countered around the perfect feeling of her head nestling beneath Rick's chin, "that I wanted you three oafs gone over an hour ago."

She let her glare fall equally on each of them. Maybe if she found the strength to hold her own against her brothers again, she'd have a shot at facing the rest of her day.

"And if you came to be an ass again." She turned to face the man standing behind her. "You can just—"

"I came to apologize for yesterday, actually." Rick pitched his voice low, for her ears only. "For that night two months ago. For all of it. I never meant to upset you, even if I do think you're capable of more than you're doing right now. I'm sorry if I've made things more difficult."

Even if I do think you're capable...

Well, that made one of them.

Except when she'd fought her way up from the nightmares that morning, she'd found herself more pissed at the memories for a change, than she was scared of them. And she hadn't taken another sleeping pill or pulled the pillows over her head to hide. Instead, she'd thought of Rick's visit yesterday. How he'd been so sure she could help a desperate single mother no one else would.

And that's when she'd dragged her raggedy self out of bed, and come up with her ridiculous plan to go into work—to face the courthouse again—for the first time since the shooting.

She pulled away from him now. From all four men.

"I'm sure I have something for that nose inside," she said to Rick. "That is, if you really came to eat crow. Just give me a few minutes to change for the office, then you can grovel to your heart's content."

"I said I'm here to apologize, Monty," Rick teased. "Groveling's a totally different thing."

She almost smiled at his familiar sarcasm.

"The rest of you," she said to her brothers. "If I see one more punch thrown, I'll call some of the lieutenant's buddies over to lock you up. Now get off my lawn. You're trespassing on private property."

She headed up her brick walk. It took way too much concentration to stay on her feet for the sake of the nosey teen peering through the sheers, but Emma got the job done.

Downing could follow or not. After her

petulance yesterday and her brothers' bully-
ing, she wouldn't blame the man for barrel-
ing out of there on two wheels. But her
challenge had been born of a need to rattle
herself, as much as her brothers.

Something had to change, damn it. Inside
of her. In her world. For Jessie's sake, as well
as her own. She was going to find fresh
stockings, something besides jeans that
would fit her shrinking frame, and she was
heading into town to look over the Sanchez
files Brad still hadn't e-mailed. How she'd
get through it all without being scared of her
own shadow, she had no idea.

But she was going to do it.

How else could she prove to herself, that she
really could escape the memories for good?

CHAPTER SIX

RICK STEPPED onto Emma's porch, finding the woman's teenager hovering just inside.

"Are you going to fight with my uncles again?" Jessie's eyes were sparkling the way her mother's did, when Emma threw down a challenge. The kid took in the blood on his T-shirt, where he'd wiped his nose on his shoulder, and smiled wider. "No one takes them all on at once. They'll probably respect you for that one day. And you didn't do too bad, even if my mom had to save your butt before my uncles beat it to a pulp."

Her excitement at the prospect of more carnage was oddly charming.

Rick laughed.

"Your mom certainly holds her own with the three of them."

The Montgomery Three were loitering at the curb now. Off the lawn Emma had banished them from, casually leaning against the cab of Rick's truck. Watching Emma wade into their fight had shaved five years off Rick's life. But even exhausted and underweight, she'd come out the victor.

"I bet those three have been protecting your mom her entire life," he mused.

The teenager's snort said she'd like to have a piece of his bet.

"She raised them," explained the kid who was as beautiful as her mother. "Not the other way around. Mom's never needed anyone to protect her before now."

The tremor in Jessie's voice made Rick blink. He gazed back at the welcoming committee waiting for him at the curb, absorbing what had been said around him over the last few minutes in a different light.

"She didn't seem to need any protection a few minutes ago." He gave Jessie's shoulder a reassuring squeeze. "I'll square things with your uncles, then I'll give your mom another chance to kick me out, too. We should all be out of your hair in no time."

His wink dragged a grin from the teen.

"Jess," Emma called from inside. "Phone Caroline and see if you can hang at her house this afternoon."

Jessie didn't look thrilled by the suggestion.

"I think I'll just stay here," she yelled back.

"I think you'll do as I ask." Her mother's tone said the discussion was over. "I'm going into town for a few hours, so why not go to your friend's and have a little fun?"

Jessie looked at Rick, worried again. Scared. "My mom thinks she can drive to work all by herself, without anyone's help."

"So that's what this was all about?"

"Nope." Jessie thunked him on the shoulder before turning away. "But you're getting warmer."

She disappeared toward the den, pulling a pink phone from her back pocket and dialing.

"Okay." Rick wiped at the blood still oozing from the cut over his eye. When he turned back to the yard, his welcoming committee straightened at the curb. "Okay."

His mind was too jumbled with contradictions and surprises to leave room for sweating the stupidity of facing the Montgomery brothers again. Not only was Emma's *baby* a teenager Emma must have had while she was still a kid herself. But the most independent career woman he'd ever met, in a town full of bright, competitive women, had *raised* three bruisers who were local fire and rescue heroes?

He held his hands up as he approached the

men, preemptively surrendering. He stopped a few feet from where the grass merged with the sidewalk. The scrapes and bruises he'd dished out made him feel a little better about the ones he was sporting.

"Your sister, who can barely stand, has decided to drive herself into town?" he asked. "And you three thought spending Saturday morning hovering on her doorstep was the way to handle it?"

"She's not driving anywhere." Charlie Montgomery whipped off his cap, then jammed it on again, bill reversed. "Doctor's orders. Even if she doesn't want us helping her, she's in no shape to be driving anywhere, let alone taking the interstate into Atlanta. She's not—"

"Then I'll drive her." The offer shocked Rick as much as it obviously did the other men. "Assuming I can talk her into letting me. It's probably my fault, anyway. I mentioned a case to her yesterday, and—"

"What the hell *were* you doing here yesterday?" Chris was the oldest, so it was fitting that he was the first to break the sidewalk-grass barrier. "What case?"

"Her office is mishandling the defense of a single mother I arrested, and—"

"And the last defendant of hers you were involved with tried to shoot his way out of court, through our sister. Why the hell would she be interested in anything you have to say now?"

Rick kept his gaze on the man's scuffed boots.

"What's the deal between you and Emma?" Randy asked. "Last night, she was furious at you and certain you were gone for good. Now, here you are apologizing and offering to help her out, after she stopped us from cleaning your clock. What gives?"

Rick stared down the woman's brothers and swallowed the impulse to ask his own questions—like what was with their sister's personal vendetta against Rick all these years. It didn't matter. Not now.

"I was standing beside your sister while that asshole threatened to take her hostage. It was my fault she took a bullet and almost died in the hospital. I'd like to help her if I can, case or not. So, I'll drive your sister to her office or to the grocery store or just around the block, if that's what it takes to get her out of that house and put some life back into her eyes. If you've got a problem with that, then let's get it on again, because all three of you together aren't enough to stop me."

Over the shocked silence that followed, the quieter of the three brothers cleared his throat and swiped at the darkening bruise on his chin.

"This is the first time we've seen her show any interest in anything besides Jessie since…" Charlie cleared his throat again. Scuffed the ground beneath his feet with boots as worn as his brothers'. "Emma says she's still in a lot of pain—"

"Shut up, Charlie," his brothers demanded in unison.

"But her doctors are saying no way. Not enough to need the amount of meds she takes. Not enough to keep her in bed all day."

"I said shut up," Randy growled.

"Not if this guy can get through to Emma," the younger brother blustered back.

"Him?"

"Whoever she'll let in, man. Which isn't going to be any of us. Not today. If Emma's determined to go into the city, and this asshole's willing to make sure she doesn't drive herself into an embankment on I-85, then I say we let him."

Rick let them work it out, while he processed Charlie's revelation, combined with his own suspicions after yesterday.

"I'll drive her, then I'll leave her alone, if that helps at all," he said over their escalating argument.

He'd apologized. He'd do it again, then he'd help Emma however he could today. If she turned out to be interested in the Sanchez situation, he'd be grateful. Then he'd bring her home and back away from the Montgomerys' world with a whole lot more finesse then he'd barreled into it, no matter how badly he needed the feel of her body against his again.

"Are you really interested in helping our sister," Randy demanded, "or is this about saving your ass and the arrest she says you've screwed up?"

Three pairs of muscled arms folded over chests strong enough to carry ladders and hoses and equipment so heavy it would drop any average man who tried to handle them.

"If worrying about this case helps Emma, then that's all that matters," Rick said. "If not, the Sanchez problem is mine to deal with. She won't hear another word from me."

He'd take care of the job on his own starting tomorrow.

Today was about a very beautiful, struggling public defender who needed to get back on track, before she let the courthouse shooting he'd bungled ruin her life.

EMMA DIDN'T KNOW what she'd been thinking.

When she'd emerged from her bedroom wearing a suit that was so big on her it was comical, Jessie had been doctoring Rick's face using the kitchen first-aid kit. It had seemed so logical in that moment. Simple enough.

Rick had offered to give her a ride into town on his way home, even though his home was nowhere near the city. Jessie had looked so relieved at the idea, and promptly promised to hang out at Caroline's all afternoon while Emma was gone. Emma would call a cab from the courthouse for the return trip, once she'd put her mind to rest about the Sanchez problem. What could it hurt? Jessie's high five, combined with the pain stuff Emma had taken after coming back inside, had made it seem like a logical decision.

Except, *logical* had escalated to *bad idea* the second she'd found herself cooped up beside Rick in the cab of his truck. And the closer they'd gotten to the courthouse, the faster downhill her courage had spiraled.

She'd stood outside the building for a full ten minutes, shaking at the bottom of the stairs that led up from the street. She'd finally had to ask Rick for even more help. Otherwise she'd still be there.

"You're obviously in no shape to be back in the office," Jefferson Caldwell grumbled from the doorway of her office.

Of course her director had chosen today to be working his first Saturday in recent memory. Jeff spared Emma his next scolding look. Rick got to enjoy that one all by himself.

"It's entirely inappropriate for you to be here at all." Jeff pointed his index finger at the hovering man. "You have no business discussing details of an ongoing case with one of my lawyers, especially one who isn't even representing the woman."

"I've done everything I could to formally discuss the Sanchez case with Mr. Griffin." Rick settled into Emma's guest chair.

He crossed his feet at the ankles, which must have been a guy thing. A self-assured, good-'ol-boy, guy thing that her brothers did with annoying frequency. Particularly when they wanted to pull off *disinterested* and *badass* at the same time.

"Your associate won't return my calls,"

Rick continued. "And he refuses to consider asking for further investigation on his client's behalf, regardless of the new information I've collected. He seems satisfied to let the charges stick."

"Investigating is your department's job, Lieutenant," Jeff lectured. "And both your chief and the district attorney are satisfied with what's been done. Your new leads are hearsay at best, and the defendant is sticking by her initial confession. She's willing to accept the five years we've negotiated in return for her plea. No matter how much the press, or you, want my office to swing at a pitch in the dirt, it's not going to happen. And off the record, I'm not exactly losing sleep at night because one of my lawyers gets to take a drug-dealing, unwed mother off the streets for a change. As long as her rights are protected to the best of this office's abilities, I'm good with it."

"What does being an unwed mother have to do with keeping Mrs. Sanchez from being mistakenly arraigned for drug trafficking?" Emma snapped.

She caught Downing's raised eyebrow at her tone.

She'd told him she'd only need to stay for

a few minutes. That she wouldn't need more than that to review the thorough history she was sure Brad had kept on the case. An hour later, they were still there. And, damn it if she wasn't grateful not to be alone while she weathered her boss's disapproval.

"Olivia Sanchez was selling drugs out of her government-subsidized apartment, Ms. Montgomery." When challenged, Jeff always reverted to formal titles.

"Was she?"

"She was using at least her youngest boy as a runner. The good lieutenant's community task force caught the kid streeting the stuff at his middle school."

Emma pressed a hand to her throbbing side. Focused through the need for more Vicodin. She kept her head down, scanning Griffin's patchy notes. But she didn't have to see Downing's face to feel his awareness of every rib-splitting breath she took.

"I see that the minor child insists the mother knew nothing about his activities," she said. When Jeff didn't respond, she looked to Rick. "Hosea Sanchez said he didn't even know what he was selling. That he'd simply been told to carry a packet of… What was it?"

"Crack." Rick winced. "He claims a friend of his older brother offered him money to take a package to another friend after school."

"You caught him in broad daylight," Jeff corrected. "Selling rocks of the stuff to a classmate."

"Yeah," Rick said. "It doesn't add up."

"Which leads us to the stash in the apartment—under his mother's bed. If the woman wasn't involved, as he first claimed, what were the drugs doing in her room, but nowhere else in the place?"

Emma flipped through the typed notes with a shaking hand. "There's nothing here to indicate that Brad ever asked that question. Nothing beyond Hosea's initial statement to the responding officer."

"Because the mother has shut the boys up," Jeff said. "No one in the family is talking anymore."

"Which means it's entirely possible the defendant is confessing to protect one or more of her children." Emma glanced to Rick for his take.

He uncrossed his legs and stood, pacing to her office's fourth-floor view of Atlanta's downtown skyline.

"Hosea refused to finger either of his older brothers by name," he said. "Though Carlos has been busted once already for possession. We never got an ID out of Hosea for the brother's friend, either. He was going to take the full rap, then we caught a search warrant for the apartment and found the stash. The mother's prints were all over it. She insisted her kids knew nothing about it, so—"

"So, job well done, Lieutenant." Jeff checked his watch, then sighed in the general direction of Downing's back. "I have a late tee time. It's good to have you back behind your desk, Emma. But if you're not ready to see things more clearly than this, maybe you should take some additional time off. The D.A. has a solid confession, and Griffin's doing his best to take care of the family in sentencing. Don't let this eat at you. There are more important things—"

"For me to worry my pretty little head about?" she finished for him.

It was like listening to her brothers all over again. And maybe they were right.

On the drive downtown, then staring at the building from outside, then every second she'd sat behind her desk, she hadn't been able to silence the echoes in her mind. From the courthouse shooting, or her childhood memories. It was as if it had all become the same nightmare. And the exhaustion of not letting the barrage of images win grew with every second she wasn't home, hiding out in her bed.

"Maybe… Maybe I should head home."

Rick's head whipped toward her at the weakness in her voice.

Jeff, as oblivious as ever to anything that didn't directly affect him, reached toward the desk, nodding. He closed the Sanchez file and took it with him as he left.

"We'll still be here, Emma, when you're ready to dive into another case," he said over his shoulder, as he left without waiting for a response.

Rick was back to staring out the window at the deepening afternoon shadows. "That went about as well as my *What the hell, boy!* conversation with my captain yesterday."

"What about that interview you gave on yesterday's news?" The interview that had had more to do with Emma's sleepless night than she'd cared to admit. Something was way wrong with this case, if the Atlanta Police Department's rising star was crashing and burning on network TV.

"I wouldn't be surprised if the D.A. wants

my ass in a cell right about now," he agreed. "Right next to Olivia Sanchez."

"Because this mess is stealing his reelection thunder?" She watched Downing bury his large hands into the back pockets of his jeans.

It was just the distraction she needed. The man's body did unfair things to denim.

"Maybe," he admitted. "Or maybe I'm taking the feel-good out of his chance to publicly bond with the police commissioner."

"The question is *why?*" She rubbed her temple against the ache throbbing there. "Why put yourself on the line like this, when it sounds as if you made a clean bust?"

Rick's eyes squinted at the corners, the way they did whenever he concentrated. Or when he stared at her the way he was now.

"You really do need to get out of here, don't you?" he asked. Three long strides, and he was beside her. "Come on, we can finish this on the drive home."

Her relief was instantaneous, at the thought of leaving and the anticipation of leaning against Rick's strength again. But neither impulse was going to get the better of her.

"Save your pity," she snapped. "We can finish this now."

"How about you save the acting for your brothers and your kid?" Rick shot back without missing a beat. "I can tell how much you need your meds. I can hear it in your voice. It was shaking a few minutes ago, almost as badly as your hands are now. It's none of my business that your brothers and evidently your doctors don't know how much you need them, so no worries. If the people in your life are too afraid of taking the drugs away from you, you can keep your crutch."

"How dare you?" He was making it sound as if—

"How dare I?" He sounded angry, but the look on his face was… Worried? Disappointed? "You're a brilliant lawyer, Monty. One of the top legal minds in the city. Hell, the entire state, but…"

He started, as if he'd just realized he'd braced his hands on the arms of her chair and was leaning over her until every word was a warm breath against her face.

"I…" he said. "I'm sorry."

"For being an opinionated ass who doesn't know what he's talking about?" she threw back at him. "Why be sorry? It's never been a problem for you before."

"I made a mistake yesterday." He pulled

back and nodded, as if he were convincing himself. "Your brothers are right. You're not up for this, but I'm grateful you've taken the time to look into the case. Let me get you home, like I promised them I would, then I'll be out of your hair. You're going to have to deal with your addiction on your own ti—"

"What addiction?" She shoved to her feet before she remembered why that would be a really bad idea.

Rick caught her, as gently as he had the day before, but there was less hesitation in the way he let her go after helping her back to her chair. There was no tingling this time, no sparks between them. Instead, there was a distance she shouldn't have noticed, but she did.

"What addiction?" she repeated.

He shook his head. "You came in today, even though you aren't up to it. You've listened, and you've risked annoying your boss. I appreciate it. Maybe I can get Brad Griffin to follow up now. And I'm glad I could help you get out of your place for a while. But you don't need my problems with this case adding to yours. If I dig up something that can officially help with Olivia's defense, I'll find a way to make someone listen. But…"

"But what?" Emma held on to the edge of the desk and pushed back to her feet. "But you agree with Caldwell and my family? Yesterday, you were all *get off your ass and stop feeling sorry for yourself and meet with the defendant.* Now, suddenly I'm too sick to get you what you need, so it's time to cut your losses. Is that what that ridiculous addiction accusation is all about?"

"Actually—" he reached for her elbow "—I think you're a whole lot stronger than anyone around you is giving you credit for, Monty. But coming back from what you've been through isn't just about strength. Otherwise someone as strong as you wouldn't need a crutch, and—"

"My medication isn't a—"

"*And,* I've lived with an addict for too long to not see the signs. My dad disappeared into his bottle the night we buried my mother, and I haven't seen the father I used to know since. And nothing I've done has made a damn bit of difference. He may never be that man again."

"I am *not* your father," she bit out, the comparison making her stomach churn.

Or was it her fear, that she really might never again be the woman Rick had known before? The woman she suddenly wanted to be, for him—Carter Downing's son!—as much as she did for her child and herself.

"Take some advice from an alcoholic's kid," Rick said. "For Jessie's sake, at least. Deal with the fear that's shutting you off from the world. Get whatever help you need, before your pain and whatever you're using to dull it take over your life completely."

CHAPTER SEVEN

I'M SUCH AN ASSHOLE.

Rick tossed from one side to the other, pounded his pillow with a fist that wanted something harder to abuse than feathers. Then he flopped to his back.

He'd been an asshole to Emma, and he should have seen it coming. Ever since talking with her brothers, then seeing the vague look in her eyes when she'd finally emerged from her bedroom. He should have punted his commitment to drive her into town, right then and there.

But he hadn't been able to walk away.

And then I was an asshole.

She hadn't said a word on the return trip to her house. She'd been hurting. Furious. Probably making plans on how best to sic her brothers on him. And she'd been in desperate need of another dose of whatever she was taking. Which in hindsight was totally understandable. She'd put her body and her mind through more in a few hours than she probably had since the shooting—because he'd needled her to. And she'd had to fight her own family just to get out her front door, that's how seriously she'd taken Rick's concerns about the Sanchez family.

But instead of thanking her and focusing on whatever he could do to make the work easier, Rick had seen flashes of his father, every time he'd looked at her. The strongest, most outgoing man he'd ever known— falling down drunk and wasting his life away, while he refused to believe he needed help. The thought of the same thing happening to Emma had pissed Rick off. And before he could stop himself, he'd laid into her.

She hadn't wanted him to help her into her house. She'd slammed her door in his face, after he'd followed her onto the porch, regardless. It had been quiet inside. Her daughter hadn't returned home yet. And Emma had disappeared into all that quiet, isolating herself again from the rest of the world.

Exactly the way Rick had found his father an hour later, holed up in his study and staring at the curtains drawn over the windows to the backyard. He'd refused to acknowledge that Rick was even there. Which should have been all the reminder Rick needed that staying away from Emma was the best thing he could do for the woman.

Except he'd caught her relaxing against his support a couple of times that morning. Looking his way when she hadn't realized he could track her out of the corner of his eye. Or had he only imagined her needing him there?

He pounded the down pillow again and kicked his way out of the covers. When the book he'd been reading did a swan dive on his toe, he cursed.

After slipping on his briefs, limping, he headed for the stairs and ambled toward the refrigerator, hoping that eating something would distract him long enough for sleep to have a fighting chance. But he stalled out in the doorway to his mother's gourmet kitchen. The kitchen she'd renovated the same summer she'd been diagnosed with the kind of cancer that exceeded its lack of treatment options only by how quickly it earned its morbidity stats. Evidently Carter had decided to rummage for late-night leftovers, as well.

Rick's old man was nursing a glass of milk—snarling silently at it in the shadows.

It was likely the only thing besides booze he'd fed his body in days.

"You've lost more weight, Dad." Rick had long ago given up preaching about AA and grief counseling. But he drew the line at ignoring the fact that his dad was slowly killing himself.

Carter grunted and took a tentative swallow from his glass.

Rick flipped on the light over the stove, then plucked Chinese takeout from the pile of leftovers he kept perpetually stocked in the fridge. Whenever his father roused himself enough to give a damn, Rick wanted there to be something around for the man to eat. He grabbed a container of vanilla yogurt, along with a can of soda, and set the former in front of Carter.

"Damn, boy." Carter squinted into the light. He scowled deeper when Rick handed over a spoon after grabbing his fork from the silverware drawer and slamming it closed. "Are you trying to make my head explode?"

Rick dived into his garlic chicken without comment and watched as his father debated between the two flavor choices before him. Bland, and blander.

Carter had always loved his food. His wife's cooking. The spicier and richer the better. Now, each new day he rushed to get as numb as he could, as fast as he could. And one of the nastier side effects of the alcohol, besides it burning holes in his liver, was that Carter had lost his taste for everything, and everyone, except his next drink.

The yogurt won out in the end.

Satisfied with his minor victory, Rick focused his attention on his own missed dinner. Minutes later, when his father stopped spooning yogurt into his mouth, Rick looked up. Carter's attention was fixed on the brutal way Rick was stabbing at the chicken.

"You trying to kill it a second time?" Carter rasped.

Rick dropped the take-out carton without comment, snapped his root beer open and gulped half of it down. He squinted through the burn and fizz.

"Is it the Sanchez case still?" Carter asked. "Or the woman Creighton was bellyaching about last night?"

Rick belched, then picked at his chicken some more. Once his father had resumed doing the same to his yogurt, Rick risked another glance and caught his old man still watching him.

"Is this going to be an honest-to-God

bonding moment?" Rick asked. "Because you think I need advice about dealing with a woman?"

Carter's spoon hit bottom. He switched his attention to the milk. "You want me to tell you again where babies come from, and why I'll take a switch to you if I ever come home from work and catch you alone in your bedroom with your girl?"

Rick inhaled root beer and coughed until his surprise settled into a chuckle that almost felt good. Because Carter was laughing, too, and his dad's laugh had always been an easy, unguarded thing.

Nothing had been easy between them in so long, Rick had forgotten they'd had this before his mom got sick.

"I think I've got the girl-boy-baby-responsibility thing down solid, thanks," he said around the carbonation, and the emotion, clogging his throat.

Carter nodded and drained his glass.

"Did you know that Jeff Caldwell and I played high-school football together?" the man asked.

Actually, Atlanta's snooty PD Director's upscale suburban roots was a bit of trivia Carter had let slide.

"He gave you a call this afternoon, did he?" Rick asked.

"Something about you and one of his lawyers holding him up getting in nine holes with the mayor. He was going to end up late for his wife's dinner party, too."

"I don't suppose your old football buddy happened to remember to invite a friend like yourself to his soirée?"

When Rick's mother had been alive, Melissa and Carter had been on the short list for every fund-raiser and power broker dinner party from Dunwoody to Buckhead to Peachtree City and beyond.

Carter chuckled at the suggestion that he'd be welcome now. "But he did wonder if there was anything I could do about my son's obsession with a case that's none of his damn business anymore."

Rick let the words wash over him. Let the truth settle deep. The same truth he'd been fighting while he tossed and turned half the night away.

He sighed and dropped the take-out container to the counter again.

"So," his old man said. "It's the woman."

"The lawyer from the courthouse shooting." One of the few times Carter had emerged from his bottle in years had been the days right after the shooting.

"The lawyer you couldn't walk away from at the hospital?"

Rick didn't bother pretending his dad hadn't read him dead-on.

Yeah, his instincts were still screaming about Olivia Sanchez's and her son's statements. But the little voice that had saved him time and time again on the streets, wasn't talking to him about the Sanchez case tonight.

"Is it guilt because she got hurt?" was Carter's next stab at parental support. "Because it seems to me—"

"Seems to you?" The reality of having Carter focused on Rick's comings and goings, even for one night, was hard to process.

Actually, it had been forever since they'd done more than grunt or hurl thinly veiled accusations at one another. The fact that his father had been aware of any part of Rick's life for the past two days, let alone two months, was hard to believe.

Rick zeroed in on his father's empty glass, and the half-full gallon of skim milk Rick had picked up at the grocery on his way home that night. His dad had been waiting up—sobering up—all night. He'd known Rick would come clean out the fridge if he had a hard enough time sleeping.

Just as he seemed to already know that helping Emma was a responsibility Rick couldn't walk away from.

"You've got to stop feeling guilty about things you can't fix," Carter said. "Like me. This damn case that's going nowhere but a plea bargain that Sanchez woman should feel grateful she's getting. This lawyer woman you keep stalking."

"Emma's not just a woman, damn it! And I'm not stalking her." Rick abandoned his chicken and noodles and rummaged for the slice of leftover pepperoni pizza he'd seen next to the eggs. He grabbed an orange for Carter while he was at it. Why not push his luck, while the pushing was good? His dad caught the fruit one-handed. Further proof that the guy's last shot of bourbon had likely been right about the time Caldwell had called to rat out Rick.

Rick shoved cold pepperoni and sausage into his mouth. Carter made short work of the orange peel and handed over a chunk. He studied a slice of orange, then popped it into his mouth. One bite, and Rick could almost see the shock of flavor spread through his dad's mouth. Carter stared at the orange as if it was his first taste of citrus, all over again. He shoved another chunk in, while Rick bit into his slice and forced his expression not to give any hint of the hope surging inside him.

Hope that would only piss Carter off. Not to mention make Rick's disappointment worse, when his father got his drunk on again tomorrow.

"Is this lawyer who's not *just* a woman interested in the case?" Carter asked after making a dent in the rest of the orange.

"Maybe." Rick kept working on the pizza. Warned himself off scrounging for more food for his dad.

Putting too much into an alcoholic's stomach was never a good idea. Didn't matter how almost-sober the guy was.

"She interested in you?"

"Hell no!" Rick bit into the last of the crust and began stabbing at the spicy chicken some more.

"Then maybe the lady doesn't warm up to being saved any better than I do," was his father's final bit of wisdom. He took his glass to the sink. On his way out of the room, he clapped Rick on the shoulder. "She's not another job for you to do. My advice—get her out of your head while you still can. Not that anything I say makes much difference these days. Just don't let me catch the two of you alone in your bedroom, or I'll take a switch to you."

Rick choked on another sip of root beer. Fantasies of feeling Emma's soft skin beneath his, her long arms and legs twisting around him and in his sheets this time, instead of the folders on her desk, began playing with his mind all over again.

"YOU'RE ADVISING HER to plead guilty!" Emma's shock echoed off the marble of the courthouse's third-floor lobby. "This is only a preliminary arraignment—for a felony charge. You can't let her throw in the towel before she even makes it to the grand jury. Not if there's still a chance she's lying to protect her children."

Emma could sense Stephen cringing beside her. But to her friend's credit, he stayed put and silent, letting her confront Brad Griffin and make the courthouse scene to end all scenes. Since Stephen was responsible for throwing her and Rick together again, blabbing to the man about her recovery, it seemed fitting that he help her contain the collateral damage. He'd even rescheduled his Monday-afternoon appointments, to stay with her and make sure she was okay. He wasn't going anywhere.

No matter how unprofessionally she misbehaved, his glare bellowed.

So, there she was, standing just outside the courtroom where she'd been shot. And she hadn't taken any Vicodin to get her through the ordeal. In fact, she'd flushed her entire bottle that morning. Being a little shaky still and a little too loud wasn't a bad trade-off. But blowing her chance to reason with Brad, now that was a different matter.

Emma squared her shoulders, determined to face the world and what she had to do without her crutch.

"Even if Olivia suddenly decided to plead not guilty—" Brad kept glancing down the marble staircase. Deputies on crowd control were holding the media's cameras downstairs until the hearing was over. "We'd advise her to waive the grand jury and proceed straight to trial. The evidence is—"

"We?" Emma knew Jeff Caldwell wasn't making an appearance, but his gift for legal maneuvering was all over this. "Do *we* have any other tricks up our sleeves for risking as little political exposure as possible?"

"The district attorney's office has the drugs that were seized in the apartment, and my client's confession. It's an airtight case. Five years is the best deal she's going to get. There's no point in—"

"Maybe it's airtight because you're not interested in looking past the obvious." Emma toned her tantrum down, and not just because her head felt ready to throb off her shoulders.

There were reporters everywhere, and after the shooting she didn't exactly blend into the courthouse crowd. More headline drama was the last thing Brad or Olivia Sanchez needed.

"Where is your client?" she asked.

"Unfortunately, she couldn't be here," Brad said.

"And you didn't ask for a postponement?" Stephen piped up, engaging in the conversation for the first time. "Your client has a right to be here while you throw away the next ten years of her life."

"There's no need for her to be here—"

"She *needs* to hear the arraignment judge ask if she understands the consequences of her plea." Stephen leaned in. "Or is giving your client the chance to rethink her options too much of a variable?"

"Family Services chose this morning for her first visitation with her kids since she went to county lockup," Brad sputtered. "It was sudden—an opening in the social worker's schedule—and it's complicated to get the boys there from their different locations. Olivia wanted to be with her children, and I saw no need to—"

"Stand up to Jeff?" Emma asked. "The visitation timing seems a bit coincidental, don't you think? I've seen Jeff manipulate the system like this before. Placate him now, but when Olivia's conviction is overturned on appeal because you were too intimidated to think on your feet, this mess is going to wind up being your fault. Trust me."

"I…" Brad blinked, fresh out of rehearsed responses.

"You're a good lawyer, Brad, but…"

But Emma suddenly felt her legs melting out from under her.

She sent Stephen a silent plea, as she let the wall bear her weight as casually as possible.

"But being a litigator," he continued for

her without missing a beat, "is about making the tough calls on the fly. Your client always comes before a fast win. The more there is at stake, the harder it's going to be to put the client's needs before the quick decision—especially a client who's given up. But you continue to be an advocate in her best interest, even when everyone else is telling you there's no reason left to fight."

That kind of unshakable priority had never been a problem for Stephen or his boss at Atlanta Legal Aid. The sheepish look on Brad's face said that the kid knew it. And there'd been a time when Emma would never have put her own need to close a case before a client's, either. Except, hadn't Saturday been about making a quick trip to get Brad on track, so something like today wouldn't be necessary?

Her anger at Rick on the ride home had had as much to do with knowing this case wasn't going to be an easy fix, as it had with his accusation that she was flirting with chemical dependency. Then she'd spent all day yesterday trying to ignore that the Sanchez arraignment was scheduled for today, and that she should be there beforehand to talk with Brad. And even now, she was focused more on reliving her courthouse nightmare than she was focused on a colleague's poor decisions.

Yeah, she was all about the client!

"Three boys need their mother," she reminded both Brad and herself. "This family's future is your responsibility, so suck it up and dig until you know exactly what's going on. Then and only then, do you advise your client on which deal is best for her situation. If Jeff starts to rant about you complicating things, deal with it. But do your job."

"And that would be what, exactly?" The guy's frustration was understandable. He was a pawn. He likely felt played about six different ways.

"Get this farce postponed." She linked her arm around Stephen's elbow, and gave up pretending she didn't need more strength than she had. "Take care of this for Olivia, Brad. Give me the chance to see if there's anything I can do to help you. If I can't, you're losing nothing by asking for a few more days."

"Give yourself time." Stephen lent his support to both Emma and her argument, regardless of his disapproval of her being there. "And make sure your client's fully aware of what her confession is going to cost her."

"I'll…" Brad shifted his shoulders and stood a bit taller. "I'll do what I can."

"Get it done." Emma tugged on Stephen's arm, needing to get out of there.

She was going to vomit if she didn't put some distance between her and the courtroom looming behind Brad. Not that what she had to face next was going to be any more palatable. Or any easier to talk her friend into helping her accomplish.

But she was going to do it. Joining the fight to help Olivia Sanchez had somehow become a fight for her own life again. And she wasn't quitting now.

"You have a visitor," the APD desk sergeant said into the phone.

Emma hadn't called ahead to ask if Rick was working that day. Whether he'd be in the precinct or on patrol. A scary, weak part of her had hoped he'd be out, even while she'd harassed Stephen into driving her over. But there she was, and Stephen was double-parked and fuming at the curb out front—for as long as it took for him to get a ticket, or for her to mend fences so she could get Downing out of her head, whichever came first.

The sergeant hung up the phone and jabbed a thumb over his shoulder.

"Follow the hallway to the bull pen." He handed over a visitor's badge. "The lieutenant's expecting you. Third desk toward the wall, second row in."

Shaky on her feet still, she refused to brace herself against the hallway wall. She'd worn sensible flats instead of the heels that went better with her simple knit dress. Certainly she could manage walking under her own steam to face the music.

Rick Downing hadn't been subtle over the last week, but he'd been honest every step of the way. And she'd been a bitch to him in return. She was still treating him like the enemy. Now it was time to settle accounts. But when she rounded the corner and her gaze settled on his dark brown hair, her knees went soft, and she reached for that support after all.

Unfortunately, at the same moment an officer she hadn't noticed sidestepped from behind her. He knocked into her, apologized, but kept moving, his eyes never lifting from the folder he was reading. Emma leaned against the wall as the world righted itself, hating the stabbing pain in her side and the growing weakness that made dragging herself outside to Stephen and begging for a ride home sound far easier than conquering the few yards remaining between her and Rick's desk.

"Monty?" His footsteps drew near. "What are you doing here? Let's find you somewhere to sit, before you collide with more body mass than Yates."

"Yates?"

She let Rick lead her to a chair. Focused on putting one foot in front of the other, and not embarrassing herself by grabbing for his arm.

Once she was sitting, Rick crouched in front of her.

"Yates is a new guy straight from the academy. He's still trying to figure out how to wade through the paperwork that comes with working a beat job. So it's really not his fault he didn't see a knockout blonde standing right in front of him, the blind bastard. We don't get many visitors back here."

"Oh." She rubbed at the chill bumps that had sprouted on her arms, even though the *bull pen* felt as steamy as a locker room. "I didn't… The sergeant up front said it was okay to come look for you…."

"No problem. When he said a lady lawyer, I don't know what I expected. But it definitely wasn't you. Not after Saturday. Everything okay?"

Rick's smile warmed up the worry in his eyes. Worry she'd put there, along with his obvious confusion.

It was time to accept that he didn't know anything about his father's involvement in her past. But that hadn't stopped her from punishing him for it. She was *still* throwing blame at him.

"I… I just wanted to tell you in person how sorry I am for the way I've behaved. You're right to be concerned about Olivia Sanchez and her children. Whether she's guilty or innocent, I don't think my office is doing the most it can for her defense."

Not that it was technically *her* office at the moment. Jeff Caldwell's *a few more weeks of rest* had been tantamount to Emma's one-and-only warning to butt out. Which she clearly hadn't.

"I don't know if there's much more I can do to get Caldwell to dig up Olivia's real story," she admitted. "But I—"

"Caldwell's an ass." Rick smiled to take the sting out of his words, then sobered. "And he knows you're smarter and more talented than anyone else in the PD's office, including him. He's out of his mind to shrug off your questions the way he did Saturday, even if…"

"Even if you're as concerned about my current physical and mental state as my boss and my family are?"

She'd blamed Rick for seeing what she'd refused to until now. The way the pills made it okay not to fight. The way they were taking her away from the people she loved. The fear that she could lose control of them, and that maybe she wanted to.

"You were right, you know," she said. "Everyone was. I hadn't realized how numb I'd let myself become."

"You're doing great, Monty. I'm sorry for dragging you into my problems. But look at you today. You look stronger already." He sounded so sure.

Proud, almost. And there was heat in his gaze, when it landed on the heartbeat pounding away just above the neckline of her simple, navy shift.

She jerked her attention away, while her light-headedness worsened.

"It might not be a bad idea, still, for you

to take some more time off before dealing with the courthouse."

"What happened to you telling me to get off my butt and stop abandoning my clients?" She shifted away from him. "To stop hiding in my medication, before I can't find my way out?"

"I've been an ass, too. You were sick and dead on your feet Saturday, but you stood up to your boss. You fought for a client you'd never even met. I think you rock out loud, lady. You deserve to take all the time you need to get better before— Hey…you okay?"

Of course she wasn't! She couldn't see for the tears blurring her vision. Rick waited for her to pull herself together. He leaned closer, giving her a little more privacy from the rest of the officers milling around the bull pen. She took a deep, calming breath and tried to say something, but had to stop several times.

"You're doing great," he insisted.

"No, I'm not. But, thank you for believing I could do you some good with Olivia Sanchez, no matter how much I can't seem to get better myself."

"The case is my problem. My mistake to fix, if I've made one. In fact, I'm on the way over to county lockup in a few minutes. The Sanchez kids are seeing their mother today."

"I know. I just came from her arraignment, and—"

"Her what?"

"The Sanchez arraignment. I convinced Brad Griffin to—"

"You went to the courthouse again?" Rick's thumb wiped away the lone tear trickling from the corner of her eye. "That must have been hard."

A jolt of awareness zinged through her, everywhere at once, leaving her needing more. Sitting there with Downing, she realized she felt safer than she had since… since he'd held her hand in the hospital after the shooting….

"I…" *Focus on helping the client, Emma.* "I got Brad to postpone making Olivia Sanchez's guilty plea, but—"

"He was still going to plea her out?"

"That and request that the judge skip the grand jury and proceed directly to a directed verdict."

"They've got that woman convinced she should just give up!" The softness that had hypnotized her was gone from Rick's expression, but not from the touch of his fingers still stroking her cheek.

"It's possible she *is* guilty," Emma cautioned, when she'd glared at Stephen for suggesting the same thing on the drive over. "Brad may simply feel this is the best way to push the district attorney for a deal—cooperating and not wasting the court's time."

"You mean, Jeff Caldwell thinks it's the best way to play his relationship with the D.A. and the press," Rick snapped.

There was a time when she'd have snapped in return, out of reflex. But Rick wasn't the enemy she'd needed him to be all this time. He'd protected her with his own life. He was helping yank her back on her feet, no matter how much the yanking hurt.

"I talked Brad into asking for a continuance," she said. "But I'm sure that'll send Jeff to DefCon 1. I may not have bought you much time. I wonder, if…"

She couldn't seriously be considering…

"You wonder if, what?" Rick asked.

"I…" Her entire body was shaking, she was so exhausted.

"You're dead on your feet again," he said. "Let me talk with Olivia one last time, while her kids are there. Maybe that will help her to see what she's giving up, if she really is lying to protect one of them. Head home and let me—"

"But I…" *I've lost my mind.* "I know I'm not her lawyer, but maybe I could…"

Rick rocked onto his heels, finally understanding.

"It would be great to have you there with me, Monty. But… Are you sure? I know I don't understand everything you're dealing with. But if the added stress of—"

She reached for his hand. He flinched, then squeezed her fingers.

"You do understand." She glanced around to be sure no one gave a damn about the two of them, which of course they didn't. "What you said Saturday, it really made a difference. I've gotten rid of the pain pills, and—"

"Is that a good idea?"

"I made it to the courthouse this morning, without my daughter calling in the cavalry. I made it over here." She took a deep breath. "I'm still on the antianxiety stuff, and it doesn't feel good yet. But it feels a little better, thanks to you. And I wanted to let you know, over and above the case, that…well…I'm sorry for…"

"Stop apologizing. You don't have to—"

"I do. I wasn't angry at you, but I took it out on you. And I've done that before, a lot, because of…" Because of stuff she had no intention of getting into with Rick. *Ever.*

"Because of things that don't matter anymore. Things that were never your fault. So—"

"Really, it's okay." Rick had that uncomfortable look a man got when a woman was about to bawl all over him. "You don't have to—"

"Would you just let me apologize!" She dropped his hand and punched him in the shoulder.

He rubbed the spot and chuckled, the sound and her outburst drawing the attention they hadn't rated before.

"You're trying to help a family," she said. "And you were trying to help me…."

"Apology accepted," he offered, even though his frown said he didn't really understand.

"No matter how complicated things have been between us, you made me think. And you made me want to—"

"Punch my lights out?" His smile was back.

"Yeah, that, too, but—"

"Emma, if anyone had a reason to hide for a while, it's you. I'm happy you're doing what it takes to get out into the world. But I want you to be okay. No case is worth jeopardizing that. I want…"

He didn't finish, and a part of her was glad not to know any more about what he wanted.

She'd apologized. He'd accepted. They'd made their peace. The end.

At least that should have been the end.

But there was a new kind of admiration in the man's gaze. And there was a new kernel of peace, somewhere deep inside Emma, that she didn't want to examine in the middle of a police precinct.

And there was Olivia Sanchez, waiting to see her kids....

Rick stood, his fingers sliding from hers. He helped her to her feet, then stepped away. She braced a hand on the chair, refusing let herself need more of his support.

"So what do you say?" she asked. "Can I tag along with you to county?"

Her knees were mush. Her side felt like throbbing fire. But she was finishing this.

"Are you sure?" Rick glanced at her death grip on the chair.

"No." But a woman was facing the exact same fate Emma's mother once had. Only this time, thanks to the son of the man who'd taken Emma's mother away from her, there might be something Emma could do to stop what was happening to the Sanchez family. "But I'm doing it, regardless!"

CHAPTER EIGHT

THE LOOK ON STEPHEN'S face promised trouble, but that didn't stop Rick from helping Emma down the precinct's granite steps. Creighton rushed forward when Emma's knees nearly buckled at the curb.

He was a bulldog of an attorney, and an excellent poker buddy. But the man's fancy law degree and family money aside, Stephen's dangerous edge was high on Rick's list of things he wouldn't want to tangle with, without a damn good reason. Stephen flipped open his phone and began dialing.

"Your brother's been trying to reach you on your cell," he said.

Emma tried to stop him. "I turned the ringer off because—" She gasped and would have toppled onto the guy if Rick hadn't caught her.

"Randy?" Stephen said. "Yeah, she's right here. Hold on."

Emma shook her head at the offered

phone. Rick grabbed the thing, ignoring the way she stared as if he'd just poured water over her kitten.

"Montgomery?" he said into the receiver. A succinct curse answered from the other end. "Yeah, it's great to hear your voice, too. You can blame this one on Creighton. I had nothing to do with getting Emma here, but I'm sure as hell not going to look a gift horse in the mouth. So if you want to bawl me out for helping you keep an eye on your invalid sister again, I should have her home in a couple of hours."

The next curse was Stephen's. Rick closed the phone on Randy Montgomery's tirade and tossed it to his friend.

"Invalid?" Emma's pale cheeks blushed with color.

"Are you trying to get us both beaten to a pulp?" Stephen demanded.

"Emma wants to go to county with me. You can drive her over, but you can't get her into the meeting she wants to observe. So why don't you head back to your afternoon appointments and let me keep an eye on her for a while."

"What meeting?" Stephen asked.

Rick waited for Emma to answer. To be sure. Whatever she decided, he'd support.

"I'm…" Emma glanced at him, then faced

their mutual friend. "I need to speak with Olivia Sanchez, and Rick's agreed to help me."

"You mean, you need to meet with another attorney's client," Stephen corrected. "So you can pump the woman for information without counsel's consent? Not a good idea, even if you weren't so—"

"Pitiful?" she sputtered.

"I never said you're pitiful."

"Well, even if I am, I'm a grown woman. And I'll go wherever I want, any damn time I want, without you or anyone else *keeping an eye* on me!"

She directed the last bit of her rant at Rick, reminding him that Emma Montgomery, angry, was a gorgeous thing to behold. It was good to see her spunk returning.

Really good.

"Might as well head to work, man." Rick gave Stephen his best *know-when-to-fold-'em* grin. "The lady knows her own mind, even if the men in her life are tripping all over each other telling her she doesn't."

Rick *was* waving a red flag in front of the Montgomery brothers, and he'd managed to piss Stephen off to boot. But he didn't give a good damn at the moment. He'd had to dry his old man out again that morning before he'd headed into the precinct. He had a full day of paperwork to finish before he returned to parole tomorrow. Stacked up against all that, Emma's cadre of male mother hens didn't make a dent in his stress level.

"The *lady's* standing right here," Emma insisted. "In case you two have forgotten."

Rick found her thunderous expression perversely erotic. Evidently, anything the woman did would turn him on. She was fire and silk. A wicked combination.

"Lieutenant Downing can drop me home once we're through," she insisted to Stephen.

"You're still on leave," Stephen cautioned. "What do you think you're going to be able to do at county, when—"

"I'm going to do my job."

Rick trailed behind Emma as she marched away from Stephen and his sleek BMW, wondering if he'd ever understand what made her tick. Something had shifted between them at the precinct. Her unnecessary apology. Her offer to help with Sanchez after all. The way seeing her again, touching her, had instantly soothed Rick's lousy day. Being with Emma was one surprise after another, and he'd be damned if he'd let that go a second before he had to. He turned the corner of the building, toward the gated area where the squad cars were parked. As he'd expected, the starch went out of Emma's spine as soon as she was beyond the other lawyer's sight line. Rick caught her arm, adding just enough support to keep her walking, her head held high, her tattered control firmly in place.

She was fighting, instead of quitting. It was an amazing transformation from just a few days ago. Hell yeah, he was willing to drive her across town, and grateful to have her help in the bargain.

Fire and silk…

Helping the Sanchez family had become a way for him to help Emma, he realized. She'd become important to him in a way nothing had since his mother had died, and his father had given up on living, too.

Damn.

And Rick had thought watching her get shot was the most terrifying thing he'd ever experience in his life!

"GET OUT, BOTH OF YOU!" Olivia Sanchez demanded.

Rick sat between Emma and the irate Dominican woman.

"This lady's from the public defender's office," he explained. "You and your kids can trust her. Tell her the truth and let her help you."

"I already have a lawyer. I got all the help I can handle."

Emma saw the grit of a street fighter in Olivia's tough jawline, even if the woman seemed too young to have a half-grown child, and too scared to be standing up to Rick the way she was. There was nothing fiercer than a mother protecting her young.

"Like there's anything anyone in this city wants," Olivia ranted on, "'cept a scapegoat for the drugs they can't keep outa my kids' hands! It's a way of life where we come from. It's all over you people's suburbs, too, but it's my family that's gonna pay. Because my neighborhood's where you come looking first, Lieutenant. How's a new lawyer gonna help with that?"

Rick absorbed her accusations without flinching. He'd no doubt heard them thousands of times. More than once, when Emma had questioned him on the stand. "The city police and county sheriff's departments work every day to protect everyone's kids from the drugs pouring into the city. Your children are what's important here, Olivia. Keeping them with you, and out of trouble. If you'd give us permission to speak with Hosea again, maybe Ms. Montgomery—"

"Talkin' to my boy's not your job!" Olivia's fist pounded the scarred aluminum table. "You done your job. I'm locked up here. You got no business trying to pile more trouble onto Hosea."

"No one's trying to single him out for anything he didn't do," Emma assured her. "But he is facing possession charges, for the incident at school. He and your other boys are with Family Services, because you're taking responsibility for the drugs in the apartment. But that doesn't jibe with Hosea's story, that the drugs he had came from one of his brothers' friends."

"I got no control over what that child said. But none of my boys have nothin' to do with the shit you cops found in my place."

Emma could feel Rick holding back, waiting for her to use some lawyer's trick to make the other woman tell the truth.

"Your statements don't add up, Olivia. And Lieutenant Downing can't uncover the evidence we'll need to keep your family together, unless you're willing to make this situation right."

"You're not my lawyer, bitch." Olivia pulled her hands from the table and crossed her arms over her chest. "You stay away from my children. Both of you. Don't go putting ideas into their heads. I speak for this family. Where are they? Why aren't my kids here yet?"

Emma was the enemy. She got that. Any lawyer would be. And Olivia was fighting for survival. For her family. But Emma was the best around at reading cagey defendants and getting through to them on whatever level worked. And after fifteen minutes, she still had no idea whether or not she could trust this woman.

"Typically they hold minor children in another room first, especially if they're coming from several different locations. Supervised visitation is timed, and it's easier to control the duration when everyone's coming and going at once."

"Typically? Easier?" Olivia squinted, as if she were peering at something slimy she needed to scrape off her shoe. "Lady, you got no business here. There ain't nothing typical about me and my boys, or any other family in the projects. You go on back to your sidewalks and lawns and parks that get mowed by the city. And to the schools where your kids actually graduate and go to college. Hookers and pimps work my neighborhood. My kids' schools don't teach them nothin', but why stealin' or dealin' is better than anything they learn from a book. I don't give a damn about making anything easy for you or them folks who got my kids."

"How about easier for the children?" Rick asked. When Emma nodded in encouragement, he leaned closer to the woman he felt responsible for locking up. "Your boys are scared and upset. I've sensed for a while that they're saying what you're telling them to now. That you think taking responsibility for the drugs and not letting my department investigate further is somehow going to—"

"Those drugs were mine, like I said. There's nothing to investigate."

"Emma could help, if your story did change. She could maybe work out a deal with the district attorney's office, that could make this better for your entire family, if you'll just—"

"I saw your boys on the news the other night," Emma pressed. "They're beautiful. You've obviously worked hard to do right by all of them. And I know that's not easy for a single parent. But you keep resisting Lieutenant Downing's help, even though you say you're doing it for your kids. You're going to lose all of them over this, Olivia. Whatever secrets you're keeping, there are other ways to protect Hosea and his brothers than going to prison, so other people have to raise them."

Olivia said nothing, but her body language was getting more hostile by the second.

"I promise you," Emma said, "I'll protect your family every way I can."

She heard herself claiming the case. Rick's attention jerked to her as she did it.

"I've reviewed Hosea's statement," he said to Olivia. "And—"

"You leave my son alone!" Olivia was on her feet. "I'm pleading guilty to the charges. I'm not changing my story. Now get out, or I'll—"

"You're facing felony charges with extreme minimum sentences." Emma sounded harsher, less empathetic than she'd ever been with a defendant. But she couldn't help it. So far, she wasn't screaming at the woman to make her see reason, so that was something. "Your file says there's no family to take care of your children. A guilty plea is taking away the only option you have."

"I got no options," Olivia insisted.

"You could fight!" Emma's anger was out of context and nowhere in the vicinity of professional, but did this woman think giving up was really what was best for her family?

What kind of mother just gave up?

Rick inched his chair closer to Emma's, while her past slid further into the present. She could feel it bubbling beneath her crumbling composure. If he touched her, she'd lose it completely.

She dropped her hands from the table to her lap.

"When you go to prison," she continued, "Children and Family Services most likely won't be able to place the boys together. Five years is a long time…" *It might be forever,* Emma's mind intruded, just as it had been for her mother. "Once you're paroled, you'll have a felony conviction on your sheet. You'd have to convince a Family Court judge that you're ready to be a better parent to your child before you could get Hosea back. The older boys will be grown by then."

Emma braced her elbows on the table again. Her temples were pounding. Even though she knew she was still sitting in the chair, she could no longer feel it beneath her.

"Lieutenant Downing…" she muttered. "Maybe he could explain the rest…."

Rick's hand found hers, grounding her while her vision clouded even more.

"Mama!" a squeal intruded as the door to the interview room burst open.

A flurry of motion followed as all three Sanchez boys burst into the room and swarmed their mother. A Children's Services caseworker Emma should have known by name followed, hovering just out of reach.

Emma realized she'd left the table and Downing's touch behind. She was pressed against the wall, as far away from the touching reunion as she could get. The children showered their mother with hugs and rough, little-boy kisses. All while Olivia, so lippy and hard-edged just moments ago, burst into tears and hauled them closer. She promised it would be okay, no matter what happened. That she'd make sure her babies would be okay.

I promise, Emma, I'll be out as soon as I can, but this is for the best… I have to protect you and your brothers… Until I get out, you're in charge of the boys…I promise…

"You gonna let my mama go now?" Olivia's youngest son looked so fierce, with his arm protectively wrapped around his mother.

He stared Rick down the way a man three times his size would.

"I can't, Hosea." Rick stood to face the young man. "Not unless there's more evidence. Testimony that clears her involvement."

"She didn't do nothin'!"

"That's not what she's telling her lawyer. How can you be so sure?"

"He's not," Olivia barked at her son. "You shut you mouth, boy."

"But—" Hosea argued.

"You got nothing else to say," Olivia insisted.

"You can trust me and Ms. Montgomery here," Rick assured the child. "A lot more than you can trust whoever dragged that junk into your apartment, your mother's bedroom, and gave it to you to take to school. Just tell us the truth, Hosea, and maybe we can get your mother home to you and your brothers."

The boy shot hatred toward Emma. "Who the hell are you?"

"I…" Emma glanced at Rick. "I work with the public defender's office. Your mother's in very serious trouble, Hosea. If you know anything that could help clear her, Lieutenant Downing's the right person to talk to."

"No!" his mother argued. "I decide what the cops hear. End of story."

Hosea's scowl deepened, but he nodded at his mother.

Failure wrecked Rick's expression, while Emma's mind faded to another room almost exactly like this one, where her own family had fallen apart.

Don't take my mom away!

Mom, tell them they're wrong. Tell them to stop!

"Let's give them some privacy," someone was saying. A hand pulled on her arm. Rick's hand. "Monty? You okay?"

"Get away from me," she said at the same time she realized she was crying.

"Emma?" He tried to grab her arm, but she was already stumbling toward the door.

Away from him and the family scene that was ripping her heart out.

"I said, stay away from me!"

CHAPTER NINE

RICK SPRINTED out of the interview room, after an Emma Montgomery he'd never seen before.

This Emma wasn't the spitfire who'd grilled him on the stand countless times. She wasn't the helpless mother he'd held, bleeding, in his arms while she begged for her daughter. She wasn't even the ghostlike waif who'd opened her front door to him a few days ago.

This Emma was terrified. She'd grown more and more agitated as the interview went on. He'd understood her fear at the courthouse, but she'd toughed her way through it. What was there to spook her at county?

He made it down the hall, to the common area where family and guests were staged before visitation. Emma was running now, weaving on legs too weak to handle it. A gaggle of press had assembled, apparently tipped off about the Sanchez family reunion and hoping for juicy coverage to pump up the five o'clock news.

Emma, a high-profile personality ever since the shooting, ran blindly toward them.

"Ms. Montgomery!" The closest reporter shoved a microphone in her face, his body blocking her access to the door she'd been sprinting toward. "Are you here in an official capacity?"

"What?" Emma blinked into the cameras and lights. She tried and failed to dodge the man.

"Are you now defending Mrs. Sanchez against the charges Lieutenant Downing and the APD arrested her for? Is she changing her guilty plea? Has Bradley Griffin been removed from the case? Are you replacing him?"

"What? No. No one's… I…"

"Ms. Montgomery is here in a nonofficial capacity." Rick took her arm. "She has no comment to—"

"Lieutenant, are you still pursuing the hunch that Mrs. Sanchez is not responsible for—"

"No comment." The microphones were in his face now.

He steered Emma around the seething

horde, using his body to shield her. The questions kept coming. Louder. More demanding.

"Ms. Montgomery—"

"Lieutenant Downing—"

"Is this meeting why the Sanchez arraignment was postponed this morning, or—"

"No comment!"

He hustled Emma through the nearest door to a restricted area, hoping he wasn't hurting her in the rush. His uniform got them buzzed through to the hallway where detainees were processed before returning to lockup. The clamor of voices followed, but only until the heavy door swung shut.

Rick stopped. Emma struggled to keep going.

"Wait," he said.

She pulled harder to get away. At least she tried. There wasn't much fight left in her.

"I know you're upset, and that scene didn't help." He pulled her around to face him, but she wouldn't look him in the eye. "Wait a second, and I'll—"

"Let me go." She yanked free. Stumbled. Actually tried to kick him as a reward for his help.

"Knock it off, Emma." He held up a hand to stall a nearby guard who was heading their way. "Quiet down, or you'll have your very own cell to cool off in. The guys behind this door don't fool around. You're assaulting a uniformed cop, and that's not going to fly in here. Breathe and calm the hell down."

Focus crept into her eyes. Then they filled with tears that threatened to take *his* legs out from under him.

"I…" She bit her lip. "I…I'm sorry."

"Just hold on for another minute." He led her to the closest room that would give them some privacy, and then to a chair. He moved out of reach, but made sure he was standing between her and the door he'd left open. "Try and take it easy. The press will hit the road eventually, once they realize there's nothing left to see."

But Emma's breathing didn't calm. Her eyes glazed over. It was like watching an addict fall into the nirvana of his next hit.

Except Emma was off whatever she'd been taking Saturday. She'd been fine since she'd shown up at the precinct. Hurting and exhausted, but fine.

"Hey?" Rick knelt in front of her. "It's okay. As soon as the cameras and reporters are gone, I'll take you home and you can get some sleep. For now, you don't have to—"

"I have to get out of here…" Her pupils

were dilated. Her breathing so quick, she couldn't seem to take in enough air. "Your father…my mother…"

"My father? What does he have to do with any of this? Emma—"

Rick's phone vibrated. He checked the display and cursed when he saw his father's number.

Carter?

The man never called Rick's cell.

Rick ripped the thing open, while he kept a careful eye on Emma. "Dad, this isn't a good ti—"

"I'm ass first in the tomato plants, damn it." Carter's voice was strained. Vague with booze. Brittle. "What timeisit? When…when the…hell are you coming home?"

"What's happened?" Rick was already helping Emma to her feet. "Are you hurt?"

"Damn rrrake…" his father slurred, "keeps tripping me…when I try to…to get up…"

"Then stop trying to get up."

Rick pictured his father with a broken leg, in a drunken midday stupor tripping over and over, on a rake he couldn't focus on long enough to move out of the way.

Another curse accompanied the sound of a bone-jarring thud.

"I'll be right there, Dad. Don't move."

Rick slapped his phone closed. His parent's Dunwoody home was twenty minutes away, *if* downtown and interstate traffic cooperated once they pushed their way out of the building.

"I'll take you home," he said to Emma as they walked back toward the outer door to the common area. "But I need to make a stop on the way."

"Stop where?" she asked.

"At my father's."

Where Rick prayed she'd stay in the car.

"DAMN SSSHHHOES." Carter kicked at the dirt under his tennis shoes and let loose every curse he could dredge up. Pain shot up his leg as a reward. "Goddamn rrrake."

He was a bumbling fool. Kept tripping, then tripping again. Had to call his kid, 'cause he was drunk. He was useless to his boy. Nothing but trouble anymore.

"Dad?" Footsteps closed in from the direction of the house.

Carter had left the side door open when he'd gotten the bright idea to weed the remaining tomato plants, after keeping Jim Beam company all morning.

"Dad! Where does it hurt?" Rick's concerned, exasperated expression came into view as he knelt beside him. So did the pricey pumps and mile-long legs of the woman he'd brought with him.

"Just get me to my—my feet and get the hell out of here!" Carter yelled.

The woman knelt, too. Rick's lawyer lady? Body language said she didn't want to be there any more than Carter wanted the audience. Her face was turned up to Rick's, but there was something familiar about it. Something Carter should have recognized, not that the bourbon he'd drunk was interested in letting him.

"Maybe you shouldn't move him until you're sure nothing's broken," the broad said.

"There ain't nothin' broken, lady. Now— Ah!" Pain zinged up Carter's leg, from his ankle to his knee this time.

"It looks like it's just a sprain." Rick was rotating Carter's foot. "Nothing to worry about."

"Dammmmit," Carter yanked his leg away. "Stoppokin' an proddin. I'm fffine. Just can't s-standupis all. You gonnahelpmeup, or you gonna sit there talkin' about it all afternoon!"

"Okay, Dad. Up you go."

Rick's arms hooked under Carter's. One yank, and Carter was standing. His one good leg bent under the strain of bearing all his weight. The other was throbbing like a son of a bitch.

Not that Carter was feeling anything much as Rick braced one hand on his shoulder, while he used the other to help his lady friend up until Carter was eye to eye with the memory he hadn't been able to set his mind on before.

The blurry image of another woman wavered into focus. A dead woman he'd helped the Atlanta legal system screw over in one of his least finest moments on the force—over a decade ago.

She just stood there, her familiar eyes teary. Her expression wrecked by pain and hatred. Or maybe she wasn't there at all. Maybe Carter's ghosts had finally claimed what was left of his pickled brain.

"Dad, this is—"

"Montgommmery," Carter hiccupped out. "Jasminnne Montgomery…"

"What?" Rick checked out the ghost's tears. His hand moved to the woman's very real shoulder. "Do you need to sit down?" he asked her.

"No…" She kept staring at Carter, as if she'd be coming after his jugular any second.

"Emma?" Rick asked.

"Jasmine." Carter forced out, this time without the boozey slur. "She… She's…

"Jasmine was my mother," the ghost in his son's grasp said.

She seemed to be having as hard a time as Carter was, staying on her feet. He tipped his head toward her for a better look, and would have kept on tipping, if not for Rick's arm bracing him up.

"Little Emma Montgomery?" He rounded the question out with a whistle that his splitting headache instantly resented.

The beauty at his son's side gave a tight nod, her eyes sharpening on him like knives.

"You ruined my life," Jasmine spat at him. "*Trust the system,* you said. *Everything will be okay.* Well, it wasn't. And you don't even remember, you bastard!"

"No!" Carter backed away, tripping over the dead bushes he never should have planted in the first place and going down again.

"Dad!" His son got him back to his feet. "Are you okay? What's she talking about?"

"Noth…nothing…" He pulled free and edged more carefully away from the memories his booze-addled brain had conjured up. "Nothing but me doing the job, the best way a man could. Just like you do."

The woman stared at him, her expression screaming that Carter and his best could both go to hell.

"What's he talking about?" Rick asked her.

"He's talking about fifteen years ago," she explained. "And how his best was a joke, in a room just like the one we were grilling Olivia Sanchez in. Your father's the reason my mother died in prison, Rick. He's the cop who arrested her when she wouldn't let my father kill one of my brothers in one of his alcoholic rages. Your father ruined my life."

CHAPTER TEN

THE PAST WAS CLOSING IN around Emma. She and Rick had left Dunwoody fifteen minutes ago. But stuck in afternoon rush hour, they still hadn't made it to her place, two suburbs away.

Compliments of the late-autumn time change, the sky was closer to dark now than dusk. And even if Emma decided to turn her head to look at the man driving beside her, she wouldn't be able to see much. So maybe it wasn't so rude that she could only stare straight ahead.

Her thoughts were swirling too fast, too full of the last few hours. Carter hadn't known who she was. Not really. Not through the alcohol he'd consumed. Not after so long, no matter how fresh the memories still were for her. After all, her mother had been just one more arrest for him, in a twenty-five-year career. One more trial to testify at, then forget so he could keep doing his job.

And Rick had never known. Meanwhile, her past had been eating her alive since the courthouse shooting. Like a paralyzing cloud, it covered every decision she made now. It had even wormed its way into her helping with the Sanchez case, and driven her to confront Carter Downing, instead of staying in the truck the way Rick had asked.

"Your father…" She breathed in. Out. "I…"

In that instant when they'd come face-to-face, she'd felt the horrifying compulsion to lash out at a sick old man who'd just made it to his feet.

She'd lost her grip on reality months ago, and everyone around her was paying the price.

"My father took your mother away from you…" Rick's Southern drawl had tightened. His voice was nearly unrecognizable.

There was a weighted silence, then a sigh from the other side of the bench seat.

"He arrested her?" Rick pressed.

"While she was still covered in her own blood, from my father beating the hell out of her for the second time that day. She was defending herself, Rick. Anyone with half a brain could have seen that…."

Emma made herself stop.

Forced herself to breathe.

Stop this, now!

"Your father was abusive?" Rick asked.

"And yours had come to the house five times before, because of neighbors' calls." Each time, Emma had prayed Carter would take her father way.

"Your mother never filed a formal complaint? I'm sure if she had—"

"She couldn't take that chance. My father never drank outside the house. He was the perfect employee at work. None of their friends suspected anything abusive was going on. Not even the neighbors, really. Or maybe they just didn't care, as long as the yelling stopped. Maybe that's why no one would tell the cops…your father…anything on the record…"

At some level, Emma realized she was babbling about stuff she'd never discussed with anyone. Not once. Not even her brothers.

"She thought no one would believe her," Rick surmised.

"My dad made sure of it. She got so good at hiding the truth, sometimes I think she even hid it from herself. She never left the apartment when there were bruises or cuts.

Not until after they'd healed. Us kids were never allowed to tell anyone. It was too much of a risk."

"Because if someone found out, your father—"

"Would kill one of us." That's what he'd always threatened. None of them would have been safe from the lethal rage he showed no one else in the world. And Jasmine Montgomery had been willing to sacrifice whatever she had to, to keep her children safe.

"Your mother never did anything about it?"

"You mean, like head to one of the battered women's shelters that Atlanta didn't have fifteen years ago!" Emma had gone over and over it in her mind. Making every excuse there was for how her mother had given up. "Or run with us, with no way to support her kids without my father's salary? Or run without us? Leave my brothers and me to fend for ourselves, when just the sound of one of us breathing was enough to send him into a rage some nights?"

"He was a messed-up asshole, Emma," Rick said with the certainty of any cop with years of experience on the force. He'd no doubt heard worse. Seen worse. "You're not the reason your mother stayed. And your father would have beat her, no matter what you or your brothers did."

The steering wheel creaked beneath Rick's hands. The turn signal did its thing as he took a left that brought her one crossroads closer to being done with this day, and the Downings, for good.

"So…" he asked as carefully as she'd ever heard a man ask a question. "You've blamed Carter all these years, for not talking your mom into leaving your father?"

"And I blame *me*."

She'd been the oldest. Her mom's confidante.

"But…" Rick was staring at her when he should have been watching the road. She could feel his gaze. "Is that what your problem's been with me? All this time, it's really been about my—"

"Carter was the first on the scene that night, all right!" She was ashamed of the anger. The fury toward everyone involved, who'd stood back and done nothing to stop her life from unraveling. It made no sense, especially after all this time. Randy and the rest of her brothers had moved on years ago. But she'd never been able to, and now it was all bubbling up, no matter how hard she tried to stop it. "Your father knew what had happened. He believed my mother's story. Told her not to worry, that it was clearly self-defense. Then he arrested her!"

"Yeah… Standard procedure." The leather steering wheel creaked. Rick wasn't trying to talk her out of her rage, she'd give him that.

"I told him my father was coming after my brothers with a gun—because the three of them had pulled him off my mother. They were eleven, ten and eight. My mom and I stopped him. Then they fought, and… It was an accident. The gun just went off. But Carter took her to county anyway, while another cop dragged my brothers and me to Family Services."

"He'd have had no choice…."

"No? And after his promise that the D.A. would offer a self-defense plea evaporated, I suppose he had no choice but to testify against my mother at the arraignment, either? Then the trial."

The same way Rick enthusiastically testified against every collar he made.

"That's an officer's job, Monty. You know that. But I'm sure Dad told the jury exactly what he saw. If that wasn't enough to help her defense make their case, then…

"My mother's public defender was useless! The district attorney ate the man's Fruit Loops with every witness, including your father. Every bit of evidence suddenly gave my mother motive, premeditation. He made the jury think she'd antagonized my father into his anger. That *she'd* brought the gun into the fight."

"It was her gun?"

"My grandfather had registered it in her name, but it had been decades since she'd touched it. My father kept it with him whenever he was in the house. He locked it in a safe when he left. He was aiming it at her, then me. Then she reached to take it away and it…"

Bile crawled up Emma's throat.

Panic.

The past rushing closer.

"Your mother was trying to save *you*, wasn't she?" Rick asked. "Not your brothers."

Ever since the Tanner Simmons shooting, the truth had been churning and festering and looking for the crack in Emma's control that would finally set it free. Then, when she'd looked into Carter Montgomery's face again after all these years…

"The gunshot was so loud…" she said in the same whisper that was all she'd been able to manage when she'd given her statement to Rick's father at the scene. "She…my mother screamed when she realized she'd killed him. I… I… We thought she was going to kill herself. My brothers…" The words burned on their way out. "Charlie and Chris wrestled the gun from her. The prosecution even used *that* to make it seem like the boys were worried she'd hurt them, too."

"Shit," Rick said. "You were—"

"Seventeen."

A part of her would always be seventeen and alone. Watching the violent home life that had been the only security she'd ever known die right in front of her.

"But if you witnessed the whole thing, and you gave your statement…" He stopped.

His long, silent stare said he didn't want to believe what she was about to tell him. That he was finally understanding what had happened to her at county that afternoon, while she'd been powerless to keep Olivia Sanchez from making the same mistake Emma's mother had.

"My brothers and I gave statements at the scene," Emma said. "But my mother refused to let us testify during the trial. There was no evidence to support anything but a bad fight and four kids who'd do anything, including lie, to keep their only living parent out of prison. No formal complaints about other beatings. No medical records to substantiate the injuries. The gun was hers and the gunshot residue was all over her hands. The forensic pathologist, the crime-scene guys, your father's report… She was guilty. Why would anyone listen to us kids? So—"

"So she sacrificed herself to keep the four of you out of it, just like Olivia Sanchez seems to be doing for her family."

Emma tried, but she couldn't get another word out.

It wasn't until she'd squeezed the fingers her hand was curled around, that she realized she'd reached for Rick. That he was trying to comfort her, no matter how much hate she'd thrown at him because of his father's role in her screwed-up past. He was staring out the windshield again.

"You heard my father's testimony yourself?" he finally asked.

"I was in court that day. My mother had finally caved, and agreed to let me take the stand. I was older. I'd convinced her I could handle it. Carter recognized me when I came into the courtroom. He looked so guilty. But he did his job on the stand."

"He mentioned the other visits to your house?"

Emma nodded. "And that there had never been grounds for an arrest. He seemed sorry about it, like he cared. But that didn't stop him, or the prosecutor from making the most of his testimony. Once he was done, there was no reason for me to get up in front of everyone. At least that's what my mother's PD told her. That was the day the prosecution offered a plea."

"Involuntary manslaughter?"

Emma nodded. Focused on the feel of Rick's thumb rubbing across her hand. It suddenly seemed as if Rick was her anchor in the present. His touch was all she had to hold her there.

"The judge agreed to a sentence of three to five years," she said. "My mother was supposed to have been out in as little as eighteen months. What a bargain. Your father… My mom asked to talk with him one last time. She'd been so dependent on my dad, mean bastard that he was. And I guess she couldn't… She didn't know how to make that kind of decision without a man's help. And she'd known your father for years, while he patrolled our neighborhood. So, she asked Carter what she should do."

"Damn!" Rick's curse slapped at the darkness filling the truck's cab.

"I was there, in the interview room. Carter assured my mom that eighteen months would go by fast. That the boys and I would be taken care of. Then the social worker came in to take me away... I didn't want to go. Your father... Carter helped her drag me into the hall. Evidently we made quite a scene. I didn't really remember it until..."

"Until today," Rick finished.

She and her mother had clung to each other, while Jasmine Montgomery promised she'd do what she had to, to get them all back. To end the nightmare for good.

Emma could almost picture her meltdown when Olivia Sanchez finally got to see her boys replaying in Rick's mind.

"We saw my mother one more time," Emma found a way to say. "All of us, at her sentencing. Then..."

"Then she died." Rick raised Emma's hand to his lips. Gave it a kiss.

She should have pulled away and stopped making this his problem. But she couldn't. Just as she couldn't hate him anymore. Maybe not even his dad. Somehow, over the last week, Rick had become what she'd needed to get through the memories—instead of being a reminder of what she had to beat away at, so she could keep forgetting. Now everything was pouring out, and he was there still, making sure she wasn't alone in the darkness.

"It happened just one month in," she heard herself say. "Before we even had a chance to visit her. Some fight over turf in the workout yard or something. She was in the wrong place at the wrong time. She never should have been there at all…."

"How long were you and your brothers with Children's Services?"

"Over a year. The boys, anyway. We had no close relatives, no one who'd take us." The boys had gone to two different group homes. Chris and Randy had been placed together. Charlie on his own. "When I turned eighteen, I rolled out of the system and got two part-time jobs. An apartment. It took me six months to prove I could care for my brothers on public assistance."

"And then you raised them. Put yourself through college and law school…."

There was admiration in Rick's voice, when he should have been resenting the hell out of her for the unfair grief she'd given him over the years.

Images from the day's dizzying events circled closer. All of it, too real. Being at the courthouse again. Being part of that drama at county. Finally facing the man she'd blamed for so much, and seeing him broken and human and suffering himself. Not the devil after all.

"Emma…" Rick sounded as if he was about to apologize.

She couldn't think of anything more impossible to handle.

"Let me go," she begged. "Please."

"Emma?" A knock on the driver's window scared a squeal out of her.

When had they stopped? She peered out the windshield. When had they reached her house?

"Get your hands off her, Downing!" Another sharp knock jerked her attention to Randy's scowling face outside Rick's window.

"Emma, get the hell out of his truck," Chris said beside Randy.

"I don't believe this." She hadn't turned her cell phone on after leaving the courthouse, and her brothers had had hours to gear up for a fight.

Rick let loose a particularly vulgar curse. All three of her brothers were flanking the truck now. She unlocked her door and opened it. Told her body to cooperate for just a few minutes more. It was only a few yards from the curb to the house. And then it would be just her and Jessie and another frozen pizza to burn.

"Emma?" Rick stepped out on the other side of the truck.

"Stay right where you are, Downing," Charlie said at her side.

"We heard what happened at county," Chris chimed in.

"What?" Emma leaned against the cab.

"You two were all over the evening news." Randy stalked around the truck. His hand went to her elbow.

"You son of a bitch." Chris pinned Rick with a hate-filled glare. "You just wouldn't quit, until you'd pulled our sister into your mess. Are you okay?" he asked Emma.

All of her brothers looked as if they really, really needed her to say no, so they had an excuse to pound on Rick.

"Always," she replied instead. "Aren't I always okay?"

If they'd caught the mess at county on the news, then every single one of them knew she was lying. But no one moved a muscle to contradict her.

"Have a nice evening, boys." She was dragging her feet, but she was moving. She held her hand up when Randy started to follow. Her head high, she left her brothers behind, along with the man who'd helped her believe she was strong enough to return to her life today.

Strong enough to face memories far worse than the Simmons shooting. Except she couldn't. Not anymore. Not tonight. Her side was killing her, her brothers wouldn't be put off forever, and her head felt like a vacuum she couldn't pull another coherent thought from. But she needed to get inside to her daughter. She desperately needed to see Jessie.

Tomorrow. Tomorrow would be soon enough to deal with everything else. Everything, except—

"Any of you touch a hair on Rick Downing's head," she said, turning to her brothers, "and you'll no longer be welcome in my home."

She'd almost reached the front door, almost succeeded in doing at least that on her own, when she realized she didn't have her purse. Not that she needed her keys. Jessie had been home from school for hours and was no doubt watching everything from the front windows.

Footsteps approached from behind her.

"What!" She turned, expecting to find one of her brothers grimly nipping at her heels.

Rick held out her bag.

"I'm sorry," he said. "If I'd known, about your mother and my father, I…"

"Well, now you do." She'd punished him for so long. Even after they'd made love, when she'd known deep down how wrong she'd been about him. "I'm so sorry, Rick. None of this has been your fault, and I've… I promise, I won't be a problem for you anymore. Just—"

"Emma—" He reached for her, then visibly forced himself to stop. "If there's anything I can do—"

The front door burst open behind her.

"Mom?" Jessie poked her head out. "You okay? Your note said you'd be home hours ago." She took in the tense scene around her, as if she hadn't been spying. "Again? You're all at it again?"

"Wait inside like we said, Jessie." Randy moved around Rick to cup Emma's elbow. "We'll help your mother in."

Her other brothers closed ranks, too.

"As you can see—" she wilted against the door frame "—I'm all full up of people *doing* everything they can for me."

She let Randy lead her inside. Jessie and the rest of her brothers followed, leaving Rick standing outside. She'd come full circle, to where she'd been last Friday—broken and surrounded by people who didn't expect her to face ugly truths.

She would be safe there with them, her family thought. But tonight, her home felt more like a prison. And the truth was, if she didn't stop hiding, she'd never be free. She'd never get her life back. The real life she and the people she cared about deserved. The life an insane part of her could suddenly see Rick Downing sharing, if she could find some way to face how badly she wanted him in it.

CHAPTER ELEVEN

"THAT WOMAN'S BLOWN through a third of your collars in the last twelve months!" Barrette said, sitting beside Rick at the coffee shop's counter.

His call at six that morning had yanked Rick's butt out of bed and into town—even though it was Rick's day off, and he'd spent most of the night in Emergency having Carter's hip and leg x-rayed to be sure nothing was broken. Pumping him for information about Jasmine Montgomery, and anything Carter could remember about the trial or what had happened after. Then convincing Carter that he hadn't seen a ghost. *She looks like Jasmine*…the man had kept muttering.

"Emma Montgomery's the best legal mind in the PD's office," Rick insisted to his boss. "And that includes her director."

"So you decided to rub Jeff Caldwell's nose in her brilliance?" Barrette bit into his jelly doughnut and munched out a few bites of frustration. "He bitched at me all through lunch yesterday. By the time I came looking for you, you'd already hit the streets, or so I thought. Imagine my surprise when the evening news had film of you and Emma Montgomery hustling out of county, practically hand in hand." He wiped at the powdered sugar on his chin. "Reporters have been calling ever since, wanting to know if the department has any official explanation for what the two of you were doing there."

Rick counted himself lucky that his ass-chewing was playing out at Barrette's favorite breakfast stop, instead of at the station. Surely, if he was about to be suspended, it would be happening in a more formal setting that didn't smell of bacon, strong coffee and sugar glaze.

"She approached me yesterday, sir. She'd already been to the arraignment. When she heard I was headed down to see the defendant, she—"

"You taking it upon yourself to speak with Olivia Sanchez again is a subject I assure you we'll get around to next," Barrette interrupted.

"I was on my lunch break."

"I told you to butt out."

"I wasn't bothering anyone at the district attorney's office."

"You escorted the city's top public defender down to county in your squad car!"

"A PD who's currently on leave."

"Not for much longer, according to Caldwell."

"We did nothing—"

"Don't finish that sentence. I told you to stop interfering with the Sanchez case. You *do* realize what Emma Montgomery's acquittal record is against you, right? And you took her there yourself!"

Rick's coffee might as well have been turpentine, but he swallowed it. Any way he could get caffeine into his body that morning.

"If this thing does go to trial now, are you going to testify for the prosecution to make sure Olivia Sanchez is put away?" his boss asked. "Are you going to make sure her kids are placed somewhere safe?"

"Safe according to who? The D.A.?"

"How about according to the legal system?"

"Or the press?"

"Or a fragile-looking public defender, who you respect a whole lot more than you thought you did, and have been keeping tabs on since she got shot and nearly died in your arms?"

Rick chugged his scalding coffee, welcoming the burn. Whiskey would have added something to it. But Carter was proof enough that drinking at eight in the morning only invited a man's demons closer.

"Yeah, I feel responsible for Tanner Simmons shooting her," he admitted. "And for dragging her into the Sanchez mess."

Hell, what didn't he feel responsible for these days?

"Don't you think you've raked yourself over the coals long enough, man? You're a damn good cop, but even you can't fix everything."

"I'm not trying to fix her." Rick pressed his thumbs into his closed eyelids. Hell, he just kept hurting her all over again. "And I'm not trying to blow the Sanchez arrest. I'm just trying to get to the truth."

And the truth was, losing Emma Montgomery from his life was what he couldn't keep his mind off that morning, not helping Olivia and her family. Rick had battled Emma in court. Made insane love to her. Protected her with his body. Held her hand when she'd coded in the hospital. Listened to her face the horrible memories eating her up inside.

And last night, it had felt as if he'd watched a part of Emma give up.

"You're really not going to be able to let this one go, are you?" his captain prodded.

The case or the woman? Carter had asked.

When Rick didn't answer, Barrette wadded his napkin into a ball and dropped it onto his plate.

"Well, I guess I better get going, then," he said.

"This is political crap, Captain," Rick finally said. "A lot of good people could get hurt if we let this case slide so we don't inconvenience a few political officials."

The Sanchez family *and* Emma, because she'd no doubt feel responsible if those boys went into the system now.

"We?" Barrette slanted his eyes and waited.

"I need as much time as you can give me, before you take me out of commission," Rick said. "Olivia Sanchez is acting cagey, but there's still a chance I'm right about her confession. And any chance is worth pursuing. I can't quit digging until I'm sure. Not with kids involved and the kind of public momentum that family has working against them."

Barrette's inventive curse cracked Rick's first smile of the day.

"You're a class act," Barrette said. "Just like your old man. And normally, I'd give you high marks for following your instincts. But I have to ask. Which is more important to you—helping this family, or helping the woman you've dragged into this with you?"

Rick stared into his mug. "Have you been talking to Carter?"

"He been after you about her, too?" Barrette had been Carter's partner the last fifteen years of Carter's career. "Is he doing that much better?"

"He's up and down. Maybe a bit more up the last few days." The few times he'd roused himself to worry about Rick's growing obsession with Emma and the case.

"He loves you, kid," Barrette said. "No matter how badly he's lousing things up now."

"Yeah."

Love.

Rick couldn't remember the last time he'd slowed down long enough to believe in whatever someone else thought was love. Except maybe the day of the shooting, when Emma had begged him to take a message to her daughter. The desperation in her eyes had shaken him. Almost made him jealous. A part of him had wanted her to need him that badly, even then.

"Carter would do anything in this world

for you," Barrette pressed. "That's what parents do, even fall-down-drunk ones."

"And mothers facing a felony conviction?" Mothers like Jasmine Montgomery and Olivia Sanchez.

Rick was more certain than ever that the Sanchez family was covering something up. And he was even more committed not to bail on his investigation until he was certain what that *something* was. For the Sanchez family's and Emma's sake.

Barrette sighed.

"I'll hold off on reacting in an official capacity for as long as I can," he promised. "But you've got to keep the press out of whatever you do next. Take a few days leave if you need them, but stay off the media's radar. Stay in an entirely different time zone, if you have to. The next time the Chief's bothered enough to call me and ask what the hell's going on, you'll be suspended. And your career…"

"You got leverage enough to protect yourself in this?"

Rick was willing to take the heat. Maybe Carter was right. Maybe Rick was losing it and begging to be taken down. But he wasn't taking Barrette with him.

"Guess *we*'ll just have to worry about that when we get there." The captain dug for bills and change in his uniform pockets.

Before he struck pay dirt, Rick tossed a ten onto the counter to cover the meal. Barrette nodded and stood.

"Of course," the man added, "it wouldn't hurt if you and your instincts could manufacture a miracle or two. Maybe find something to help these people while you make the district attorney, the PD director *and* the department look good, all at the same time."

A pat on the shoulder later, and Rick was sitting alone, contemplating his cold coffee and untouched doughnut.

He couldn't talk to Hosea without his mother's approval. Getting in to see Olivia under the media's radar would be impossible now. Caldwell would toss him right out of the PD's office if Rick were stupid enough to show his face there again. And before Rick went anywhere else, he had to stop by home and try to get his *loving* father to eat something to counteract the booze that was going to kill the man one day, no matter how hard Rick fought to stop it.

On top of that, he needed to see Emma again. Was she better that morning? Damn, he missed her, even if there was no way she was missing Carter Downing's kid in return. Not after everything she'd told him last night.

Yeah, he was a regular miracle man.

"YOU TOLD ME I wasn't ready for court yet." Emma covered the end of the cordless phone with her palm, so she could be as quiet as possible about banging her throbbing head against her kitchen cabinets.

"Yes." The strain wearing Jeff Caldwell's voice thin said he wasn't exactly doing a happy dance on his end of the line. "Because you looked ready to collapse at my feet Saturday, and you were worked up about a case you knew nothing about. But none of that stopped you from pulling rank on another attorney, or postponing an arraignment the press was panting to cover. So I'm thinking I may have underestimated you a bit."

"I'm sorry, Jeff. I was going to call you first thing this morning." Once she'd had enough coffee to make herself coherent, and more than fifteen minutes to figure out what she wanted her next step to be. "I know I stepped over the line yesterday, but—"

"You pole-vaulted your way into the

middle of this case." He pounded his fist against what sounded like his desk.

"I wanted to observe the hearing—"

"What hearing? You played on Brad's loyalty to you, got the thing called off and then marched over to county so you could make an even bigger scene with the defendant and her kids. What where you thinking?"

"I…" She hadn't been thinking. "I…" She cleared her throat. "I—"

"You're the new lead on the Sanchez case," Jeff repeated.

"That's not a good idea, and you know it. I stepped over a line with Brad Griffin, and I'll do whatever I can to help him rectify the situation, but—"

"Your face was splashed all over the local networks last night, and you weren't exactly a low-profile personality before this, Emma. Not after your shooting. The office is swamped with press calls wanting to know your next move. It seems all of Atlanta thinks you're the perfect choice to fight for this family. No one else in the office will do. So guess what, you got the gig!"

"Jeff, I'm not… I don't think I can… The courthouse… I mean, yesterday, I…I didn't handle it very well."

"You'll do it. With your family history, I never would have picked you for the lead, even if you were healthy. But you've dragged yourself on board. Now deal with it."

"My family?" Everything inside Emma that had felt as though it was moving forward that morning, suddenly took a huge step back.

"Your mother. The press is going to have a field day, once they dig her story up. I'm surprised they haven't already."

"But…"

But what? He was right. Very few people knew about her past, because she liked it that way. But any researcher with half a brain, after yesterday's scene at county and studying the Sanchez case history, could have the details on file and ready to print by midday.

"You really didn't think any of this through, did you?" Jeff finally sounded like the man who'd recruited her straight out of night school, instead of an angry boss who wanted her fired.

"I'll do whatever I can to help with the press," she said, "but taking on a courtroom again…"

"I know it's going to be difficult, but I don't have a choice. Once the press digs into your past, I'm going to have to spin things so that it looks like your own family's experience is exactly the reason I think you're the best choice for the job. I won't be able to downplay things after that. I'll need you here and on top of the case by then."

Emma reached for her second cup of coffee since waking up.

"I was up half the night trying to figure Sanchez out," she said. She hadn't taken the sleep meds. And her mind had refused to turn off, no matter how exhausted she was. "The woman is definitely lying, but I couldn't tell you what about, or why, yet."

"Then I suggest you find some answers," Jeff advised. "Fast."

"My gut feeling is that there's more going on with this family than the mother's admitting. The best I can tell you is that Rick Downing's hunch feels right on the money."

Rick… Her regret for every confusing thing she'd said or done to him—and his father— had been her constant companion through the night. And one of the first things she knew she had to deal with, once and for all, today.

"Your gut feelings are legendary in this office," Jeff admitted. "But you never used to let them sway your professional judgment. Not until you were sure you had a defense you could sell to a judge and jury."

"Brad was planning to skip right over exploring his defense on this case," she snapped. "So I'm not that far behind his learning curve."

Her boss sighed. "This mother's future is on the line," he said. "You've postponed her best chance at a favorable sentencing, and you've brought your own baggage into the equation. I give your family's story twelve hours, tops. If you and your brothers don't lead the eleven o'clock news, I'll buy lunch at City Grill tomorrow."

"Tomorrow!"

"Take today. Pull yourself together. Do whatever you have to, to find that fire I hired you to throw at every case. By tomorrow, I need you to be full-on Emma again. The entire package. If you're not fronting this case by then, I'll look like a fool. And—"

"Jefferson Caldwell III is nobody's fool."

"Damn straight," said the cutthroat lawyer who'd merged his commitment to defense litigation with his drive to play Atlanta's political scene to the hilt. "Get all over this case. Win it, plea it out, but do it like a rock star. And for the record—no further investigation will be requested by this office re-

garding Olivia or Hosea Sanchez's statements. Not unless you have something more
tangible to present me than your gut feeling
that there's more to dig up. Stay away from
the press. Stay away from the police. Get
yourself in here in the morning and do your
job, Emma."

Or she needn't worry about coming back
to work at all, he left unsaid.

"I'll meet with Brad first thing tomorrow,"
Emma said as Jessie stumbled into the
kitchen to guzzle orange juice straight from
the carton. "Once he's briefed me, I'll try to
meet with our client before lunch—"

"Don't try. Do it. City Grill, one o'clock.
I'll want a full briefing by then. Pull it
together, Montgomery."

"Tomorrow?" Jessie asked as Emma hung
up.

"That's how long I have to get my head out
of my ass."

Not to mention getting her mind around
what she needed from the man who'd still
been there in her early-morning dreams.

"And you're planning to do that how,
exactly?" her daughter wanted to know.

"Good question, honey."

It was a very good question.

"THIS ISN'T a good idea, Mom."

Jessie eyed Emma's keys, as if the teen was calculating the precise distance between her and them. She was coiled and ready to spring into action, if need be.

"I'll call Uncle Randy," Jessie threatened. She was dressed for school and should be getting ready to meet her bus. But she'd cornered Emma in the kitchen, instead, and now she was blocking the door to the garage. "He said you exhausted yourself yesterday, and for me not to—"

"Not to let me out of my own home without permission from one of my brothers? You have to get to school, honey, and I don't need your uncles to babysit me. Rat me out to them again, and you're grounded."

"The *doctor* said you weren't ready to drive," Jessie argued, her expression pure teenage defiance.

"True enough." Emma pined for the days when her offspring had actually been afraid of her threats. "Because of the pain meds, which I'm not taking anymore."

"No more sleep stuff, either?"

"Not last night. I'm fine, at least to drive." She pulled a soda from the refrigerator, popped the top and drank down the bubbles and caffeine and sugar, never needing the powerful mixture more. "Besides, it doesn't matter if I'm fine or not. They're expecting me at the office tomorrow."

"You collapsed at the front door last night!" Jessie snagged her own can.

"I was drained at the end of a long day. I'm better this morning." Actually, she had the emotional hangover to end all hangovers. But she siphoned the last of her cola and smiled through her panic at what she was contemplating doing. "I won't be gone long. Don't worry."

"What's so important that you have to bust out of here so early?" Jessie returned to the fridge for another soda, opened it and handed it to Emma. "Is it that cute cop who brought you home, maybe?"

"Maybe you should work on the French project that's due at the end of the week, until your bus gets here."

"Most of what I have left is a lot of reading," Jessie said. "I could do it in the car and go with you wherever you're going, then you could drop me at school later. My first period's study hall, anyway."

The kid was toying with the rim of her own can, her head angled down as if she didn't really care. But Emma could hear the fear in Jessie's voice. Without the sedatives numbing everything, it was getting easier to tune into other people's emotions, the way Emma had always been able to before.

"Look at me, honey."

Jessie tossed back the jet-black hair she'd gotten from the father she'd never met. Emma's own green eyes peeped up from behind trendy bangs.

"I'm okay," Emma assured them both at the same time. "I know the last month or so, I haven't been there for you, but—"

"You've been hurt."

Emma sipped her new soda. "I've been hiding."

"From what?"

"From a lot of things I'll never let keep me away from you again."

"You've been right here, Mom." Jessie scooted around the kitchen's cluttered center island, until Emma could see the too-high hem of the new jeans the kid was already growing out of. "You haven't gone anywhere. I didn't mind—"

"Taking care of me? That's not your job, sweetie. It's not your uncles' jobs, either."

"Nobody minded, Mom. We…" Jessie gave her the sweetest teenager cuddle imaginable, her arms thrown around Emma's shoulders and her head buried in Emma's freshly washed hair. "We almost lost you. No one cares how much time you need to come back from that. As long as you c-come back."

Emma tilted her daughter's head up, her own breath catching. She cleared the roughness from her voice.

"But you *haven't* always been sure I would. Not completely, and I'm sorry for that. Today, I'm going to do what I have to, to make everyone a little more confident that I can."

"By doing what?"

"Facing the part of my life that's *really* been scaring me all this time." Lord help her. "I've got to slay some old dragons, so maybe stepping into the courthouse tomorrow won't scare me as much as it did yesterday. And so I can start doing what I need to be doing around here for you. For us."

Her brave Jessie was trembling.

"How…how scary was it?" she asked.

"To be shot?"

Jessie's childlike nod told Emma just how badly her daughter had needed to ask the question.

"It was pretty scary." The terror had been

there in every dream Emma had had since. "But the truth is, it's not the scariest thing I've ever faced in my life. Losing my mother… I know firsthand how scary that can be, honey."

Jessie hugged her tight again, then quickly let go.

"I never thought I was going to lose you," she insisted.

"Not even a little?"

Jessie had been at the hospital the day Emma's blood pressure bottomed out—from unexpected internal complications after her surgery. The doctors had shocked her heart into beating again. Randy had said Jessie had broken down when she heard, after being so strong through everything else. She'd screamed at anyone who'd suggested that she go home and rest. For three days, Jessie had waited in the lobby, until they'd moved Emma to a private room where her daughter could sit with her and hold her hand and start to really believe Emma was going to make it.

"I…" Jessie lifted her soda, but didn't drink. "I can't imagine what it must have been like, losing your mom like you did. Being alone that way, without even your brothers at first."

"You wouldn't have been alone," Emma insisted. "Not with your uncles here."

"I know."

"But I was plenty scared, the same as you. And a lot of that fear's still there."

"Because you came so close to dying in the shooting?"

"Maybe." Emma shrugged. "It's more like—"

"Being scared of living?"

Of not getting her life back. Ever. Of never really getting back what she'd lost fifteen years ago, and of depriving her daughter of the same security.

"Something like that," she hedged.

"And whatever you're doing this morning's going to help you not be scared anymore?"

Emma thought of the shock and hatred that had consumed her when she'd faced Carter Downing after so long. The horrible things she'd said, and the answering confusion and hopelessness reflecting back from the man's eyes.

She was going back over there under her own steam. She was going to take responsibility for her memories, and her part in keeping them alive for so long. And this time, she was closing the door on the past for good.

"I sure hope so, honey." She turned toward the garage, determined to confront Carter Downing before she lost her nerve. And to hopefully avoid seeing Rick there, while she was doing it. She'd been enough trouble to him already, no matter how much more she seemed to need him fighting by her side with each passing day.

"Let's get going, then." Jessie's arm looped through Emma's. Her smile said she was either tagging along, or calling her uncles.

Emma hesitated, then nodded, letting her daughter help the way Jessie clearly needed to, and secretly grateful for the company.

CHAPTER TWELVE

"DAD?" RICK'S FIRST STEP inside the house was more of a trip, as he stumbled over one of his father's gardening loafers, then the hand trowel beside it. "Damn it. Dad?"

The man had been digging in the dirt again.

Rick headed for the garden. A clink from the direction of the kitchen had him taking a sharp right toward the sound. So, Carter was drinking again, but inside at least. The day was looking up.

Then the aroma of cooking bacon registered. And… Waffles?

A familiar laugh, then a woman's voice, had Rick quickening his pace, until he was pushing through the kitchen's swinging oak door.

"What the—"

"Hey, Lieutenant Downing," Jessie Montgomery chirped from her perch on a stool at the marble-topped island. She was watching the electric waffle iron do its thing. "Are you hungry?"

"Son," Carter groused, sober and irritated and slouched at the kitchen table.

But if Rick wasn't imagining things, there was a glint of amusement in his father's eyes. The man was still in his pajamas, but the knees were grimy with potting soil. He was nursing a steaming cup of coffee, while the sun streamed through the window over his shoulder, accentuating the lines and wrinkles the last five years had added to his face. The pasty color of his skin. But his eyes were alive—mocking Rick's detour home to make sure he was okay, as well as the activity going on over Rick's shoulder.

Rick knew who would be there when he turned around. But he didn't turn, until he was certain he could keep his expression neutral and his hands to himself.

Emma looked even more tired than last night, if that was possible. But instead of resting at home, there she was, wearing his mother's apron. Cooking for the man she'd cursed the last time she saw him.

"You came over to…make breakfast?" he asked.

"To apologize," she corrected.

Jessie hopped off the stool and grabbed the pitcher of orange juice Emma had been mixing from frozen concentrate. That's when Rick realized the kid was doing most of the work, while her mother concentrated on staying on her feet.

"She seems to think she ruffled my feathers yesterday," Carter explained, "when the two of you dragged me out of the dirt. I told her, what with me being responsible for her mother going to prison and all, I didn't mind the cold shoulder so much. Hell, she can feel free to keep hating me all she wants, as long as she leaves me the hell alone."

"How about warm waffles instead?" Jessie plopped a plate of buttered breakfast pastry in front of Carter, handed him a fork and a bottle of syrup, then sat across from him to watch him eat.

"You did your job as a cop the best way you knew how, Dad," Rick said.

"Like I've been a father to you since your mother died, the best way I know how?" Carter traded staring at Emma as though she were a ghost to fussing with the melting pats of butter. A stack of crispy bacon, just the way he liked it, had come with the Montgomerys' peace offering.

"Breakfast was Jessie's idea." Emma gave Rick plenty of space while she slowly walked to one of the island's stools.

"You'll hurt my mom's feelings if you don't eat," Jessie urged Rick's father, her smile impish. "She's been sick a long time. You wouldn't want to hurt her feelings, would you?"

"Jessie!" Emma sputtered.

But damn it if Carter didn't dive in. Grumbling, he took his first bite. Then, as if he'd never tasted anything better, he rushed a bigger forkful in the second time. Then a third.

Rick realized his mouth was hanging open and snapped it shut.

"I haven't been able to get him to eat anything before three in the afternoon, since I moved in here."

"When was that?" Jessie asked, returning to her mother's side.

"Too damn long ago," Carter mumbled around a mouthful of bacon.

"Five years," Rick corrected.

Carter glared between Emma and Jessie. "You two get your jollies harassing old men, is that it?"

"What he means is, thank you," Rick translated. "But—"

"Don't worry." Jessie gave Emma a gentle hug. "All of my uncles are snarly until after breakfast, too."

"It's lunchtime, damn it!" Carter slammed his fork down and eyed the glass of juice Jessie had brought him. He caught Rick's narrowed glare and sighed while he sipped, then coughed.

"Thank you," Rick repeated to Emma. "But this isn't necessary. You had every right to hold a grudge about what happened to your family. No one blames you for—"

"Making every time you were called in on one of my cases all-out warfare?" she asked.

Rick couldn't help smiling.

"I don't know," he said, keeping it light while heat sparked between them. "I kind of had fun taking you on in court. You give as good as you get, Monty. Comes from handling your brothers all these years, I'm guessing."

She swallowed. The confusion in her gaze deepened. Then she glanced behind him, toward Carter.

"We should be going." Emma pushed from the stool with the care of an old woman.

"I'll show you out." Rick reached for her elbow, but she edged away.

He made himself walk to the door and push it open. Jessie stayed close to her mom. He followed both of them to the front foyer.

"I'm really sorry if I upset Carter again," Emma said, once they were there. "That's not why—"

"Upset him?" Rick handed her the purse she'd left on the piano stool his mom had always used as a plant stand. "You… Carter's eating. My mother used to make him breakfast every morning. Since she died, he hardly ever comes into the kitchen, and only then, usually to get ice for his next highball. What… How did you get him to let you in here, let alone sit and watch you cook for him?"

"I rang the doorbell." Emma's smile slipped free, as she stood there, with the smell of waffles and bacon tugging his favorite childhood memories around them.

"And I told him my mom wasn't mad at him anymore, not about her mother," Jessie added.

"I made the mistake of filling her in on the way over." Emma didn't quite meet Rick's gaze as she explained. "There was no stopping her, not once she got it into her head that cooking for your father was the perfect peace offering."

"I told your dad that my mom would hold a grudge forever if he didn't let her do something about how loud his stomach was growling when we got here."

"Carter and I were both badgered into breakfast," Emma admitted. "It's Jessie's favorite meal. She's been able to make her own for years now."

"Negotiating prowess must be hereditary," Rick teased.

"Nope." Jessie opened the front door. "But not taking no for an answer is."

She disappeared outside, leaving Rick alone with her mother.

Alone with Emma Montgomery.

Last night, Rick would have bet serious money that wasn't ever happening again. Now he could feel her breath kissing across his skin as she exhaled slowly.

"What are you really doing here?" Rick asked, needing to know before she ran from him again. "You were exhausted last night."

"I was so unfair yesterday—to both of you. You let me tag along with you to county, and I can only imagine how much trouble you're in because of that. Actually I don't have to. Jeff Caldwell had me on the phone first thing this morning."

"Yeah, I'm off duty today, but my captain called me to the mat anyway. The news coverage isn't going to let up for a while, for either of us."

"My leave's been rescinded." She almost sounded relieved. "This is my last day off."

"And you decided to spend it here?"

"Actually, I decided to come back and see Carter sometime around four this morning."

"So, you're…"

"Burying ghosts, I think. I've got too much to fight for in the here and now, to be holding on to things I couldn't handle feeling when I was a kid. Things that were nobody's fault but *my* father's. But I… I'm so sorry that I—"

"No more apologies, Emma." Not that Rick wouldn't mind standing there, listening to her for as long as she wanted to keep talking.

He couldn't get over how different she seemed. This wasn't the always-confident counselor he'd known before the shooting. But she wasn't the terrified woman who'd run from the meeting with Olivia Sanchez yesterday, either.

Emma nodded, and started to turn toward the door.

"Caldwell mustn't have given you too hard

a time," he said, not wanting her to leave yet. "You seem…better."

"There's still a lot of pain." Her half smile drew him closer. "But I'm starting to feel again. It's a trade-off."

"It's good."

"I think so." She glanced over his shoulder toward the kitchen. "Some things take more courage to face than breakfast with the enemy, but I'm getting there."

Courage.

There wasn't anything sexier in the world.

"You're one of the bravest people I've ever met, Monty. Yesterday was—"

"A meltdown, I know." She turned away.

"No, it was—" He stopped her, his palm cupping her elbow. "Inspiring. You faced the courthouse. Your memories about your mother. My father… And here you are again today. You've got balls, Emma Montgomery. And you've got heart. Most people go their entire lives trying to get both right. "You're… amazing…."

She blinked, strength flickering in and out of the doubt he hated seeing in her eyes. Strength and something more. Something he'd have read as sexual need, if it were coming from anyone else.

Then the woman who had every reason in the world to walk away from him for good—the woman he now knew he'd lost his heart to, the one and only time they'd made love—grabbed fistfuls of his T-shirt and pulled him into the kiss he'd dreamed of since touching her again last Friday.

Emma was in his arms. Her scent, her taste, fired his need for more.

Amazing wasn't even close to the right word for how she felt against him. The woman's daughter was outside. His father was somewhere in the house, steaming about having his midmorning binge postponed. But Emma was trembling, nuzzling his lips, moving closer.

And there was no way Rick could let go.

Every wicked courtroom fantasy he'd had since stripping her naked on her desk was a living, breathing reality in his arms. He cupped her snug little bottom and lifted her to her toes. Combed his fingers through all that thick blond hair and held her mouth beneath his, holding off the next kiss until her green eyes opened for him. They were sparking with the same emotions raging through his body.

Need.

Passion.

More.

He took the next kiss. Stretched it. Gave in return, until her hands were roaming his back. Her nails scraping until he groaned. She nibbled his chin, then his jawline, her teeth not gentle, thank God, even when they captured his earlobe.

"Harder," he whispered, forcing his hands to stay gentle on her tiny frame.

They'd been animals the last time, and they'd have that kind of abandon again. He'd die without it. But for now, he trapped her head in place, his knees nearly buckling when she nipped the skin on the side of his neck.

"Damn, Monty. Harder. Please…"

"Rick…" she breathed into his ear, her whole body shaking. "I…"

"You okay with this?" *Please be okay with this.* "If you need—"

"I need you to keep kissing me, damn it!" She shoved him away, suddenly revving up to being pissed off. "I've got brothers to baby me, Rick Downing. A daughter who rode over here with me because I'm not fit to drive. I don't need more coddling. If you don't want to—"

"Oh, I want to…." He curled the fingers of one hand under her chin, his thumb brushing her plump lower lip. "I wanted you every time you slapped me around in court, Monty. And every day since you let me love you in your office, no matter how much you tried to ignore what we'd shared. I wanted you last night. And I wanted you this morning when I walked into my mother's kitchen and found you being kind to my father. But—"

"But what? I'm so fragile, that you think—"

"No, I don't think you're—"

"Going to break? Come on, Rick. You—"

"Damn, woman! I'm just trying to be a nice guy, and make sure you're sure."

When silence was her only response, he crushed his mouth to hers again, forgetting everything but the taste of Emma. She wasted a halfhearted second trying to turn her face away, but then her body curled closer. Her tongue feathered across his lips. Her heart pounded beneath his palm. He teased his fingers around her breast and drank each answering shiver and sigh.

"Amazing," he growled against her lips.

Monty, blossoming in his arms. Strong and healthy and fighting for more of him, instead of trying to get away.

"I…" She kissed just below his ear this time, and he nearly lost it on the spot. "I hadn't felt anything in so long," she whispered, "until you banged on my door. I told myself I wasn't coming to see you this morning. That it was just about Carter and letting go. But here you are, and you feel so good…."

He backed her to the wall where he could carefully brace her weight, then leaned his hips into exactly the part of her he needed to feel.

"God, Monty. I want to—"

"Mom?" The front door flew open, smacking him in the butt.

Jessie walked several feet into the room before realizing where they were. By the time she turned toward them, Rick had made himself step away from the girl's mother.

"Um… Oops. Sorry." A teenager had never sounded less apologetic. "Um…I can still make it to my second-period class, Mom, if someone wants to give me a ride."

"Right. School." Emma braced a hand on the wall. The other reached for Rick while she struggled for balance.

"Could you follow us to our house, Lieutenant Downing?" the girl asked.

"Jessie, don't start." Emma's stride was as shaky as her voice, while she covered the few feet to where Jessie's sass was crumbling into genuine worry. "I can certainly make it home after dropping you at—"

"Her doctor hasn't cleared her to drive," the kid said to Rick.

"Jessie," Emma warned, "knock it off. I—"

"When's your next appointment?" Rick asked.

"The driving restriction's not about my recovery," Emma snapped. "It's the—"

"The meds you're taking, right?" he asked. "Still, you have to get to work somehow, and if your doctor's said you shouldn't do it by yourself, then—"

"I'm fine."

"You're a woman with a temporary impairment. And as an officer of the law—" he winked at her daughter "—I would be remiss in my duties if I let you loose on the road until you've been cleared to drive. Let me help you today, Emma, and—"

"I'm fine," Emma repeated, her cheeks flushed.

From anger again, because he was trying to protect her?

From their kisses?

"I know just how fine you are." He stepped closer. Inhaled her scent. "But your daughter doesn't. And the only way you're not going to keep from worrying Jessie more is to accept some help."

Emma sighed and shrugged her purse higher on her shoulder. Jessie laced her fingers in her mother's grasp. "I'm so sorry, honey. I'm getting better. Really."

"I know, Mom."

Seeing the two of them side by side, the warmth of the connection between them, Rick had no trouble imagining how this duo had gotten the better of his crotchety old man. Emma squeezed Jessie's hand, then glanced over at Rick.

"Do you really have that kind of flexibility in your schedule?"

"I'm off tomorrow, too, as it turns out." For as long as it took, to wrap up his suspicions about the Sanchez arrest. "It's not a problem, really. Besides, my captain's put me on notice. I have to figure out what Olivia Sanchez is hiding, fast, or the Chief's going to feed me to the media. Me helping you get to and from work would give us more time to…"

"Collaborate?" the teenager asked. Jessie smiled at his raised eyebrow.

"Share our ideas," he corrected. "That is, if you're interested," he challenged Emma.

He held his breath.

"I…I guess tomorrow morning would be a good chance to run through everything you know," Emma conceded. "I have a late lunch scheduled with Jeff, to lay out my defense strategy. Maybe I can get in to see my doctor sometime in the afternoon."

"Then let me make sure Carter's settled, and I'll follow you two to your place, so we can drop off your car and take Jessie to—"

"Oh, Carter's just fine," his dad said from the hallway behind them. He marched to his gardening things by the front door, still wearing his pajamas. "You two go on ahead and take care of…whatever you need to do."

"Do you have to do that again today?" Rick asked.

"Every day, Ricky." His dad ambled away. He was still sober, thankfully. Sober, and sad.

Working in the garden always made him sad.

Emma blinked after him, as he walked toward the back door.

"My mother loved gardening," Rick explained. "Carter can't stop torturing himself about her. He can't let her go. The garden, no matter how badly he mangles it… Working in it is like—"

"Having your mom here still?" Jessie asked. She was glancing between him and Emma.

"Something like that." Rick realized that a part of him actually envied Carter his depression.

It said a lot about how deeply the man had loved his wife. Rick hadn't ever had that with a woman. The stress of the last five years had left him so numb most of the time, he'd been starting to wonder if he ever would.

Now, every time he was with Emma…

"You ready to go, Mom?" Jessie asked.

Rick grabbed his keys off the hall table and waited. When Emma finally nodded, relief flooded through him.

Sure he wanted to do right by the Sanchez family, even if his boss and his father saw his commitment as a career-damaging mistake. And no one was better to have on his side legally than Emma Montgomery.

But he suddenly realized he wanted Emma by his side, period. "Let's go then," he said with a nod of his own.

CHAPTER THIRTEEN

EMMA HAD BEEN SO CERTAIN she could handle this like a professional.

Now, waiting for Rick to drive her to her first day of work since the shooting, she couldn't keep the memory of the taste and feel of him from filling her mind. Making her want more of the dangerous, impossible things his kiss always made her feel. All night long, her body had been aching… It still was, on a morning when it had never been more imperative that she keep her energy focused on the job that, outside of Jessie, was her life.

Rick's black Dodge pulled into her driveway. Jessie's bus had left twenty minutes ago, so this time there was no teenage exuberance to distract from the perfection of the man stepping out of the truck and onto Emma's lawn. Scruffy, unshaven, he looked more ready to crawl back into bed, than to take her to work. The muscles in his chest strained against his T-shirt and leather jacket, as he pushed the truck's door shut. His jeans hugged his strong legs.

Rick caught her spying as he walked toward the house, and smiled. Emma dropped the curtains, picked up her briefcase and stood frozen, an arm half reaching to open the door. The man's smile had been her first conscious memory that morning. Her second? His heavy-lidded expression when he'd pinned her to the wall at his house, showing her how badly he'd needed her, too.

The job, Emma.

Today is about doing your job!

The doorbell rang, and she jumped. Then she caught herself smoothing her suit's skirt over her thighs, and balled her hands into fists.

Stop it!

She yanked the door open and stared Rick down, her gaze pinned on the sexy cleft in his chin. There didn't seem to be any part of him where she could look and not think of kissing him senseless.

"Let's get this over with." She punched the door lock and stomped past him, refusing to give in to her body's tingling reaction when their bodies brushed.

Rick pulled the door shut and tested the knob.

"You should really invest in something more sturdy," was his casual suggestion. "Any rookie burglar could defeat that lock blindfolded."

"Thanks." She marched toward the curb. "No doubt that will help me sleep better tonight."

Rick chuckled and followed after her.

She reached to open the truck's passenger door, but Rick's large hand beat her to it. He opened the door, and she quickly hoisted herself inside before he could try to help with that, too.

A sharp pain sliced down her side, but she controlled her reaction, or so she thought. Rick's hand brushed her waist as he fastened her seat belt for her. Her gasp turned into a flinch that was unstoppable.

"I thought we were past my help being such a terrible thing."

"Hello." She waved a hand in front of his face. "Have we met? I've never wanted anyone helping me. Why do you think I threatened to disown my brothers if they showed up this morning and made trouble again?"

Rick smiled, instead of snapping back. He closed her door, and walked around the front of the cab.

Rick Downing's smile… Her thoughts still weren't on track by the time he slid those long, denim-clad legs beneath the steering wheel.

"Yesterday was…" she tried.

Unforgettable?

Confusing as hell?

"I mean," she rambled on. "Today isn't about…"

"Picking up where we left off in my father's foyer, now that Jessie's not here to interrupt?"

Emma swallowed.

"Today can only be about Olivia Sanchez for me," she made herself say. "I don't have the energy to put into anything else, and still make it through this." Not to mention that a big part of her was terrified by how much she needed this man, and how badly it would hurt if it turned out that Rick didn't really need her in the same way. "So why don't you start the engine and let's get to work."

"No problem." He turned the key. "You're the boss. Where do you want to start?"

And that was that, as they backed out of the driveway and headed into town.

"Tell me whatever you know," she said, "that I can use for leverage with the mother. I need something to make her see that throwing herself on her sword won't make her family's problems go away."

Rick's fingers beat a rhythm on the steering wheel as he drove in silence. She'd noticed that it was something he did when he was deep in thought.

"Just spit it out," she prodded. "Otherwise we're wasting our time, and I'll let one of my brothers carpool me all over Atlanta until I'm officially no longer a threat on the road. Trust me, they were more than willing to take me off your hands when I talked to them last night."

Rick was shaking his head, but he was laughing, too. He pulled onto I-85.

"You're trying to get me run out of town on a rail, right?" he asked. "As long as you keep thumbing your nose at your brothers on my behalf, they'll keep sharpening their knives with me in mind. With friends like that…"

"You eat *tough guy* for breakfast, Downing. You can handle them." She caught herself smiling. Really smiling. "Olivia Sanchez? Hosea? Give me something to work with before I have to face Brad and Caldwell."

"Gangs." Rick contemplated the morning rush hour swarming all around them. "The word I'm hearing from Vice, is that either Olivia or Hosea, or possibly both of them, might be feeling threatened by a gang connection behind the drugs. Giving up whoever's putting on the pressure would—"

"Be a death sentence, maybe for the entire family. How long before you can confirm it?"

"Probably never, officially." Rick thumped the steering wheel with his fist. "These aren't the kind of sources who can go on the record and stay undercover. All I've got is what I hear around, and what I can piece together under the radar."

"Then there goes my leverage."

Emma had kicked chewing her nails over a decade ago. It wasn't the kind of habit that inspired a nervous client's confidence in their lawyer. And it definitely wasn't the kind of tell a defense attorney wanted on display for the prosecution's counsel. But her right thumbnail was in tatters, and she realized she was gnawing at a jagged edge still.

She yanked her hand away from her mouth.

"So…" Rick didn't look over to catalog her agitation, but she didn't for a second believe he wasn't aware of it. "The TV news didn't hold back on either one of our families last night."

"No, they didn't." Each station had aired its own minibiography. The whole sordid ordeal. Rick's father. Her mother. Emma's struggle to hold her family together. "That's how I ended up talking with my brothers. They were worried, but they were smart enough not to gang up on me this time. I didn't start out to tell them about you and this morning, Rick. Really."

"I believe you."

"They wanted to know what my plans were today, and my brothers and I made a pact a long time ago not to lie to each other. We were all we had, and we weren't going to mess that up by tossing trust out the window, along with everything else. It was the only security we had left."

Rick slowed for the exit ramp that led to the courthouse's one-way street.

"Security and trust…" He reached for her hand, squeezed it, then he let go. "That hasn't been what family's been like for Carter and me in a long time. Not since we lost my mother."

They slowed and double-parked at the curb. Rick set the flashers, to let other drivers know they'd be there for a while. Emma gazed out at the courthouse. She hadn't been totally sure if she could face the place again, no matter how much she'd reassured Jessie.

But in that moment, she realized she was okay. Because she wasn't sitting there alone, the way she'd faced every terrifying night and day since the shooting. Nights and days when she hadn't let herself turn to anyone for help.

She reached for Rick's hand. His palm rubbed across hers, and she could finally release the breath she hadn't been aware she was holding.

"I think I've been terrified every day since my mother was taken away from us," she finally said, the last of her defenses crashing down. "But I was always able to handle it, to ignore it, because other people needed me to. My brothers needed raising and structure and love and a family. Then my daughter's father wanted nothing to do with the responsibility of bringing another life into this world. And Jessie needed me to make that not matter one bit. My clients—I had to be fearless when I went to bat for them. People who had nowhere else to turn…."

Rick slowly lifted her knuckles and brushed them with a kiss. She looked into his eyes, and the morning's tension eased. Her insides became a puddle of need too quickly, too perfectly for comfort, but she refused to let go.

"You don't have to be okay all the time, Emma. That's no way to really heal. Living like that can make for a long recovery. Not being Superwoman doesn't make you a fail-ure, Monty."

She snorted at the image.

"Besides," he continued, "it's only been five days since I started being a butthead to you again. And look at you." He ran the back of his hand down her cheek, then a finger turned her face toward his smiling one. "I can hardly believe you're the same woman who opened her door to me last week. Whether you feel it or not, you look like a million bucks, Counselor."

"And here I thought cops had their vision checked at annual physicals. You're—"

"In awe."

"Stop saying that."

"No." Instead, he leaned in slowly, giving her time to pull away.

But her lips were tingling even before his brushed them. He was so gentle, this big, tough guy who could hold his own with her hard-ass brothers.

"I know how hard being here is for you, Monty. And that you still feel broken inside. But you're fighting again. Because other people are depending on you, and that's the kind of person you are. Courage like that is an awesome thing."

She closed her eyes and leaned her forehead against his. She thought of Rick, trying to support his father just as he was supporting her now, while Carter hid in his house, drinking himself into a stupor each day. Emma didn't want to give up that way. She wanted to be a fighter again.

"Actually, she said, "at the moment, I'm hiding out in my sworn enemy's truck, because I'm too much of a wimp to head inside."

"Sworn enemy, huh?" Rick's laugh felt like heaven. His fingers massaged the strain from her neck. "That sounds about right. But I've got your back, Monty. With Sanchez. Even with those overmuscled brothers of yours. No worries…I'm happy to be the enemy, for as long as you need me to be."

She tipped her face toward his. Rick's mouth met hers halfway with a growl. She wound her hands around his shoulders to do some massaging of her own.

I've got your back….

His promise whispered through her mind as she made herself pull away so she could face her day. She covered her mouth with a not-so-steady hand. Rick's gaze followed the motion, promising so much more than kisses.

"I…I need to get inside," she said. "But—"

"No problem." His easy grin made it impossible for her to leave. "Are you okay?"

She nodded. She had to do this. For herself, as well as for her client.

"I think I'm going to be okay," she said.

"You're going to kick ass and take names," Rick corrected. "Just like you have every other day you've stepped into that building. Thank God, it's not going to be my ass this morning."

"Well, the day's not over yet," she bantered back.

"I'll hold you to that tonight." Rick winked as he plucked her briefcase from the floor and handed it to her.

Tonight…

He checked traffic and opened his door, sliding out of the truck while she pulled herself together in the silence that followed. Too soon, he was at her door and opening it. Reaching his hand toward her.

"Do you need help up the stairs?" he asked.

"No, I got it," she answered out of habit. Then she really looked at the granite steps rising like a mountain in front of her. She swallowed and squared her shoulders. "I got it."

Rick didn't argue with her, the way her brothers would have. Instead, he pulled a piece of paper from his pocket and handed it over.

"This is my cell number. Call when you're ready to leave. I'll be around town all morning running down leads. I won't be far."

Emma nodded, slid the paper into her briefcase and made herself walk away from the promises of support—and tonight— that would be there when this impossible day was over.

One foot in front of the other, she made herself climb the steps under her own steam. And even though she knew Rick would still be there, watching to make sure she was okay, she didn't pause before pushing through the courthouse's revolving doors.

She could do this, she kept telling herself.

She had to.

"WHATCHA GOT?" Rick hadn't bothered shaving that morning.

His white, no-brand T-shirt was the wrinkled remains of yesterday's uniform. Perfect for a visit with his best DEA contact, who'd finally surfaced after being off the radar for weeks. Since Rick had served more than once on one of the department's drug task forces, he had contacts at all levels of Atlanta law enforcement.

Warren Dobson looked badass and bored while he switched his toothpick from one corner of his mouth to the other. When Rick got a whiff of Dobson's haven't-bathed-in-days cover, he felt better about how he must have looked to Emma when he'd picked her up in his street clothes. The spring humidity was doing its part in letting anyone within smelling distance know that Dobson blended in with his low-rent surroundings.

He scratched at his patchy beard, pulled a filthy ball cap from his back pocket and headed around the corner into the shade as he put it on.

"There are rumblings of a pretty big shipment coming in later this week." He pulled out his cigarettes and lit up as Rick joined him. "Friday, probably. Mexican. Coming in through Texas, then trucked here for distribution."

"Coke?" Rick took a wad of cash out of the tattered pocket of his favorite jeans. He handed over a fifty.

Warren exhaled a stream of smoke through his nose. Tucked the bill away in the breast pocket of his drugstore-cheap plaid shirt. "Among other things. Meth. Lots of money. Guns. A new cartel's setting up a hub, and we're taking them."

Rick took the stack of small envelopes wrapped in a greasy rubber band Warren handed over. He shoved it into his pocket, giving a nervous look around for added effect.

Never hurt to be too careful.

Inside one of the envelopes would be the fifty he'd passed Warren the last time they'd hooked up.

"What's your sting got to do with me?" he asked.

"Heard you're still trying to blow your

shot at detective by looking for where the smack from the Sanchez place came from."

"Something like that." Rick shoved a stick of gum in his mouth and concentrated on chewing. Well, chewing and wondering how long it would be before Emma called him for a ride home. The second they were alone again, he'd have her in his arms. "It was a clean bust, but something's off with the statements we took. A mother and three kids are involved. I've got to know that we're doing the right thing for the family, while we do what we have to to keep the drugs off the street."

"You've got to know, or Barrette does?"

Rick shrugged.

"Shit." Dobson exhaled another cloud of smoke.

"I'm on my own," Rick said. "But I'm still on the job."

"For now." Dobson dropped the cigarette and stubbed it out with the toe of his stained sneaker. "We got a name that might be connected with your case."

"A name from this cartel you're tracking?"

"The leader of the gang handling local distribution. He's homegrown. Cisco Romero."

Warren shoved his hands in his pockets and started walking. They never talked longer than a few minutes, maybe once or twice a month. But when the agent made contact, his information was always solid.

"He was Olivia Sanchez's former live-in," he added when Rick joined him where the alley opened onto the street. "Before he moved to Laredo."

"Let me guess. He's not in Laredo now."

Warren stretched and scratched an armpit. Two pigeons loitering at his feet took offense and flew off.

"Not with the size of the shipment he's got pulling in," the agent said. "We can't get a bead on him. He disappears when we get too close. Pops up somewhere else in town, or at one of his suburban crash houses. But my sources say that till two months ago, he was shacking up with his ex and their kids. That someone inside the Sanchez apartment had been doing more than dealing for him while he was in Texas. When the heat got too close—"

"He had to split, before he could get all of his product out of the apartment," Rick finished for him. "Damn."

"You sure the mother's protecting those kids of hers, and not standing by her man?" Dobson pushed the bill of his cap up far enough for Rick to see his eyes. "If she was in this gang with him, you've made a righteous bust after all, my friend. You get anything out of her that can help with our operation, you let me know." He slapped Rick on the shoulder before ambling on his way.

"CALL ME WHEN YOU GET this message," Rick finished saying into his cell as he entered Big Dog's Barbecue, home of the best ribs in Atlanta.

He hung up on his third try at reaching Emma at her office, and headed for his favorite booth. There was already someone eating there, but Rick barely slowed. He sat across the table from the guy, recalling suddenly why this midtown dive had become his favorite haunt.

"You remember how you used to beg your mother to bring you down here?" his dad asked. "You'd meet me for lunch on Saturdays, when I had patrol."

Carter's beer glass was half-empty, but he was working his way through an overflowing plate of ribs, coleslaw and corn bread.

"You drive yourself over?" Rick signaled Clover, Big Dog's daughter and the rock that kept the glorified pit turning out food so authentically good, it had a five-star-rating in every tourist rag in town.

"I'm legal," Carter groused around a rib.

Clover dropped off Rick's sweet tea and his check without breaking stride.

"I'll have your usual out in five," she chirped.

"You still working on destroying your career?" Carter dove into the coleslaw like a man who hadn't eaten in months.

Rick pushed his tea toward his father.

"I had a few sources to meet."

"On your day off?"

"Since when does a cop work nine to five?

"Barrette know?"

"More or less…" Rick nodded at the waitress who dropped off his own overflowing plate of everything his dad had gotten, plus the collard greens Carter's stomach evidently hadn't been up for.

"My bet's on less." His dad saluted him with the tea, then chugged half of it. "Doesn't bode well for the next time you see Barrette, does it?"

"How's all that food gonna bode for you, once you get home and open your next bottle?"

Rick didn't add that he'd pass on career advice from a man who'd started pickling his brain at his retirement party, and hadn't slowed down yet. After three frustrating hours of digging and calling in favors from every source he had, he had nothing new on Dobson's lead. Nothing to soften the effect of the development on Emma's case. And no word from Emma at all. Now he had Carter up his butt!

"It's good to see you up and out, man," he said, "but—"

"You're tired of treating your dad like he's a toddler who can't be left alone without supervision? Yeah, well, that makes two of us."

"If the parent-child dynamic between us is screwed up, it's because—"

"You think you can save everyone?" Carter wadded up his paper napkin and threw it onto the growing pile beside his plate. "For all your fast-track hype, you still haven't learned the first rule of being on the force, kid. People gotta want to be saved, before you can do much good for 'em. Try to force them to believe what you think's right, and they'll run back to the mess they've made the second you're gone."

"So, I was just supposed to leave you be. Let you give up after Mom died?" Rick shoved his plate of untouched food away. "It's been five years, and all you've accomplished on your own is taking early retirement and replanting, then killing, her garden every few weeks. You're making a big enough mess *with* me nagging at you every day."

"It's my mess to deal with. And you were only supposed to move in for a few months after the funeral, until I got back on my feet. What happened?"

"What happened? My father's an alcoholic, that's what happened. I had to come home from work and pick you up off the ground on Monday, Dad. You could have killed yourself out there. And except for me coming to check on you, no one would have known. You've run everyone else off. What the hell are you doing?"

"Whatever it is, it's *my* business, not yours. I thought you'd have gotten the hint by now."

"Hint?"

"You've got your own problems to worry about, kid." His old man was mainly moving his food around on his plate now, not really eating. "I'm not your problem to solve, and neither is this Sanchez case. Or that pint-sized, public defender you're panting after!"

"Don't talk about Emma like that." Rick pulled his lunch closer and ignored Carter's chuckle at his rush of overprotectiveness.

"You wanna talk about something else?" his dad asked after he watched Rick dive into his lunch. When Rick reached for his tea, Carter beat him to it and lifted the glass to his mouth, still laughing. "How about you kissin' her yesterday. Driving her to work this morning. What's next? You gonna fill *her* refrigerator with healthy food? Maybe offer to tuck her in at night so you can make everything in her life a bed of roses, too?"

"What was I supposed to do, Dad?" Rick dropped the rib he'd been eating and licked his fingers. "Watch you drink yourself to death and just walk out? Lose both my parents at the same time? Just live my life, and pretend I was okay with you throwing yours away?"

"Some people you just can't save, Ricky. Like this mother you arrested. Or Jasmine Montgomery, no matter how many times I tried to get her to help herself. Like her daughter, who you couldn't keep from getting shot—"

"And my father. My family!" Emma had said she and her crazy brothers never backed away from the truth, even when it hurt. Rick had been backpedaling for five years. And he was done. "You're not just pissing your life away, Dad. It's my life, too!"

The bustling noises around them silenced so suddenly, Rick's hand jerked to where his pistol would have been if he hadn't secured the shoulder holster in his truck's locked utility case before coming inside. Then he realized everyone was staring at *him*, not some unseen danger stalking him.

He turned to his father.

"I can't just forget about your mother," Carter said, his cantankerous sass finally gone. "Not even for you. And Lord knows I love you, boy. I—"

"You gave up when Mom died," Rick said, just above a whisper. Not because anyone was listening to them anymore, but because he couldn't get his voice to work any better. "Well, I'm not giving up on you. You don't want to fight anymore? Are you really ready to die, too? Then go ahead. But I don't quit!"

"I'm not quitting." Carter shoved the glass of tea across the table. "I'm *feeling,* not that you'd understand that. Since your mother's death, you've been so busy being the prince of lost causes, you got no time to feel anything of your own. You couldn't save me. You couldn't save this nowhere case. So now you're moving on to Emma Montgomery?"

"Emma doesn't need anyone to save her, Dad. She's at work again today, even though the courthouse still scares the shit out of her."

"Yet there you were, on the woman's doorstep this morning. What's that about?"

"If you're so bent on being alone," Rick snarled back, not liking the sense in what his father was saying, "what's that about?"

"It's about being family, remember!" Carter ranted.

Rick didn't have to look around to know they were once again the center of attention.

Letting it all hang out with his old man at Big Dog's—the boys at the station were going to love that, once the news got around. The few ribs Rick had eaten threatened to make a rapid reappearance. He swallowed the rest of his tea. Clover emerged from the back with a refill, taking the empty glass with her when she left.

"I'm your father," Carter's rough voice ground out. "That doesn't mean you're responsible for saving me. I lost the love of my life. Maybe there's no coming back from that, but it's not your fault. And putting *your* life on hold, blowing your career and chasing one lost cause after another, isn't going to change what I've become."

"A drunk?"

His dad looked down at his plate.

His still half-full beer.

"I couldn't handle the pain," he said. "I still can't. And I've let it suck me under. I thought about that a lot the other night, after Jeff called and I waited up to see if you'd come down to the kitchen. The years I've missed with you, since Melissa died. And I thought maybe I'd do something about it. That maybe you finally needed me, more than you thought I needed you. Then I got up the next day and started drinking all over again."

"And…" Rick had learned not to trust small victories, like Carter making it through a morning without getting toasted. Through a day. He'd even made it a week one time.

The man always reached for another bottle.

His laugh was short. Soulless. "Don't tell me a few waffles from a pretty woman and a call from an old friend about your renegade son finally have you grounded enough in life to consider dragging your ass onto the wagon for good."

"That PD of yours is all right, I guess," Carter said instead of answering the question.

"And her kid's cute as a button. But Emma Montgomery's no good for herself right now. I can see it in her eyes. The same thing's inside her, that's inside me. She's running. And she's not even sure from what. She's feeling it all, and that makes her just as destructive for you as I am, Rick."

"She's a colleague going through a hard time," Rick argued, not liking the direction of his father's logic, or how close to home it was hitting. "She's agreed to help with a case I have a personal interest in. Whether it goes any further than that, is—"

"That woman's got you spinning. You don't let yourself feel anything, and she can't stop feeling. It's a no-good mix, but you two can't seem to stay away from each other."

"Because we needed to talk about—"

"The case?" His old man settled deeper into the booth. "Just the case, is that it? You didn't kiss her again this morning?"

Rick didn't say anything for a long time.

"She… At first, it was because she was hurt, Dad. Because of me." He would never forget holding Emma, not being able to stop her bleeding, promising her anything she wanted and hoping it would be enough. "But that's not—"

"That's bullshit, is what it is. You did your

job in that courtroom, and it doesn't look like the woman's holding too much of a grudge anymore. You've tried to help her over the last week. Maybe you've done some good. But she's got to figure out what to do with her life, and you've got your own problems to fix."

Carter reached for his beer, only to stop. He wiped his mouth with his hand.

Rick had problems to fix?

"You gonna stop drinking?" he challenged his old man. "You want me to focus and get my life together? How about you? You ready to own some of the responsibility for taking care of yourself for a change?"

"You finally gonna figure out what *you* need," Carter challenged, "instead of hiding behind saving the rest of the world from screwing up? Your life being about other people 24-7—that might make you a hero down at the department. But it's never gonna be enough. It's never gonna make the empty go away. I might be a drunk, but at least I'm feeling for myself."

Rick grabbed both their bills and stood.

"I guess that's that, then." He headed for the register without waiting to see if Carter downed the remainder of his beer.

They hadn't settled anything. Not by a

long shot. But they'd talked. Trusted each other enough to say some of the hard things that had gone unsaid for a long time. And maybe that was a start.

The cash register jingled, and the sound of Emma's laugh replayed in Rick's mind. The memory came with a surge of desire.

But the troubled, determined look on Emma's face as she'd headed up the courthouse steps had sent a chill through Rick. The same chill that rushed him, each time he called and left another message, when she hadn't returned any of the others.

Emma was a brilliant litigator and the kind of fighter Rick couldn't help but admire. And he was willing to give her all the time she needed to fight her way back from everything that had happened.

But what if she was too afraid of losing again?

What if she kept hurting beyond Rick's ability to really reach her, no matter how hard he tried? Just like his father had. It had been five years, and Carter still hadn't found a way to let the hurt go. How long was it going to take Emma to get there?

CHAPTER FOURTEEN

"WHO IS CISCO ROMERO?" Emma asked her client.

Brad looked up from his notes. But the kid's neutral expression never wavered.

He'd spent the morning filling Emma in on the Sanchez case. Then he'd driven her to county for her first official interview with Olivia, and taken second chair during the meeting as if it had been the plan all along. His professionalism made Emma regret having misjudged him so badly when she'd first heard about the case.

Now, he simply jotted down the name Emma had thrown at the woman, then waited calmly for Olivia to answer. An answer that never came. In fact, the other woman hadn't spoken since being led into room.

"Is Cisco your children's father, or is he just the man who supplies you the drugs you sell?" Emma pressed, repeating the sketchy information Rick had left in one of his voice mails to her office phone.

Still no response from her client.

"My next meeting is with my director." Emma folded her hands in front of the laptop she preferred for note taking. "He wants to know my recommendation for moving forward. If I can't convince him that I believe you're innocent, we're back to pleaing out to a felony conviction that's going to land your children in the system. Even if the judge accepts the district attorney's five-year sentence recommendation, that's five years away from your kids. Is that really what you want? Tell me what Cisco Romero has to do with the drugs the police found in your apartment, Ms. Sanchez, so I can get you back with your boys."

The silent, angry woman sitting across the table, her arms crossed over the chest of her orange jumpsuit, had never seemed more out of her reach. The more Emma talked about this Cisco character, the less of a mother her client seemed to become.

"I hear Romero's a powerful man," Emma said. "Connected with a dangerous gang that works from here to Texas and back. Did he show up and move in without your consent?

Maybe you had no choice when he brought his drugs with him. Did he threaten you, Olivia? Your boys?"

"My boys aren't your job to worry about, lady." Olivia jabbed a finger toward Emma.

"Nope, they're yours. And they aren't going to see you again for a long time, if you keep this up."

"Keep what up! Francisco moved to Texas. I haven't seen the man since just before my Hosea was born."

"Are we going to get the same story if we ask your neighbors?" Emma tried to read the truth behind the other woman's distrust. Tried to see the scared mother from a few days ago beneath the bravado, while she kept her own memories of what the woman's children were going through out of it.

"Nobody in the projects gonna talk to you, lady."

"What about your kids?"

"What about my kids?" Olivia asked.

"Are your boys going to give us the same story, once they taste what Children's Services is like as a lifestyle? If they change their statements too late—after we ask for a nonjury ruling—it'll look like I'm trying to beat the indictment you pled guilty to. Not a good place to negotiate from. In short, your sons will be visiting you behind Plexiglas until you're paroled."

"*My* sons, Ms. Montgomery. My business." Olivia turned to Brad. "Are you gonna just sit there while this crazy bitch keeps this up?"

"Ms. Montgomery's the lead on your case now." Brad's tone was as calm as still water. But ice had frozen the good-ol'-boy warmth from his young eyes. "She's the best in the defense business. If she says you have a chance at an acquittal, there's nothing for me to do but file her briefs and watch, so maybe I can take care of a client one day, the way she's trying to take care of this mess for you."

"You can give up and plea out and protect your lover," Emma advised her client. "Or, you can put those boys first. Which is it going to be?"

Olivia gave no answer. No flicker of reaction. There was none of Monday's desperation, when her story had been all about how unfair this was for the kids she was protecting. Ever since Cisco's name had been mentioned, the woman's energy had turned positively cold.

What did Olivia Sanchez value most—

her secrets and her guy, or being a mother to her children?

Emma began stacking her notes, suddenly afraid she knew the answer. Just as afraid as she was that she couldn't handle it. At least not until she was out of there and hiding at home where she could fall apart in private. Long-ago echoes of a mother begging for just a few more minutes with her child made her motions jerky as she transferred folders to her briefcase.

Frantic.

Brad frowned at her, then stood.

"Your indictment hearing has been rescheduled for Friday." He helped Emma to her feet, then took her laptop and briefcase after picking up his own. "We were lucky to get on the docket again so quickly. Ms. Montgomery will be in touch before then, to finalize your plea."

Emma pressed the fingertips of both hands to the top of the metal table and waited for the room to stop dipping under her feet.

"Think about this, Mrs. Sanchez," she said. "Be sure that what you're giving up by not cooperating is worth whatever you think you're gaining."

Brad knocked on the door. A guard opened and stood aside as Brad and Emma left.

"I'm sorry," Emma said, as they signed out and wound their way through the bodies milling between them and the building's entrance.

"You did great with her." Brad shrugged off her apology. "I never could get her to open her mouth at all. At least she's hostile to you. And there's no way I'd have been able to push this hard for an innocent plea. Not with Caldwell breathing down my neck to wrap things up and a client who doesn't give a damn."

"But why doesn't she give a damn?" Emma asked.

Another shrug followed.

"Maybe she's just a bad mother," Brad said. "Maybe sending Sanchez to jail might be the right thing for everyone."

Emma stumbled to a halt. She couldn't see anything at the moment but her mother's tears and panic. Then she was rushing, walking as fast as she could toward the door.

"I'm sorry," she apologized again, grabbing her things from Brad. "I…I'll meet you out front."

He stared as she hurried away—impartial, always-on-top-of-it Emma Montgomery, losing it over a case that was so much more than just another case.

Rick's smile flashed through her mind, his assurances that she could handle this. Her body still burned from his touch that morning. Her pulse raced, then sank as she remembered her forced confidence as she'd walked up the stairs. The anticipation of seeing Rick again, once she'd proven to herself that she could handle today.

He believed she was all about courage, and ready to kick ass and take names. But if she was so strong, why was she running now, down the sidewalk and away from the truth about her client?

Why was the confusion worse than ever before, making her dread seeing him again that afternoon?

"I THOUGHT DOWNING had commandeered your transportation detail for the day," Stephen said from behind the wheel of his BMW.

Emma didn't respond. She hadn't answered any of the other jabs her *friend* had fired at her, either, ever since he'd taken her pleading phone call and agreed to pick her up at the county jail. She hadn't been able to face the courthouse again or her lunch with

Jeff. So she'd bailed on the rest of her day, and now she was clearly being punished.

She wasn't sure what was more annoying: that she was still so dependent on other people; that she was running like a child again; or that Stephen had thought Randy, who happened to be in the city that afternoon, would be the perfect sidekick for her escape to the burbs.

All she was sure of was that she desperately needed to be home, crawling into bed and forgetting. Forgetting the case she couldn't win and the family she couldn't save. Forgetting Rick and his kisses and the safety net he'd thrown her. And forgetting how in *awe* he was of her and how freaking terrified that made her feel, every time the world made it crystal clear how much of a fraud she really was.

"Why Downing of all people?" her brother asked from the front seat, next to Stephen. "You've been on his case for years. Now he's your confidant?"

"I would have driven her in this morning," Stephen said.

"I offered to when she called last night," Randy countered.

"At least she told you she was in the office today." Stephen glanced at her through the rearview mirror. "I had no idea, until she hit me up with the 'Home, Jeeves' phone call."

"She's been kind of standoffish lately, with everyone *but* Downing."

"You two wanna have this conversation in private?" Emma fidgeted, unable to find a position in the back seat that didn't pull at her side and add to the pounding behind her left eye. "Just pull over at the next exit, and I'll catch a cab home."

Neither man reacted, except to stare, silently now, out at the gridlocked traffic continuing for miles in front of them, down I-85. The traffic announcer on the radio broke in over the latest chart topper, to say that a five-car pileup at Spaghetti Junction had closed the six-lane highway down to one.

Emma and her happy escorts weren't going anywhere for a while.

"What did Rick do to you this morning?" Randy asked. "If I find out—"

"He didn't do anything." Emma blinked away tears. "Rick understood why I needed to do this, and he didn't treat me like an invalid when I asked for his help."

That was what she'd needed the most, she realized, beyond the passion and the sparks in every touch they shared. Rick respected her.

Trusted her. Genuinely believed she was the same fearless fighter he'd first fallen for. What was she supposed to do with that faith now, when she couldn't even make it through one defendant interview without falling apart?

"Then why aren't you with him?" Randy stared through the windshield. "If Downing understands so damn much, why are you suddenly shutting him out, the way you have the rest of us?"

"We just want you to be okay, Em," Stephen quickly added. "If today was too much, stop pushing so hard to face things before you're ready."

Emma closed her eyes against the expectation that she could find a way to be okay. Randy was right. The scared little girl inside her was still running—this time from Rick, as much as the doubts and memories and failure that had been swirling through her mind since the shooting.

Stop pushing so hard to face things before you're ready....

But what if she was never ready?

She didn't just need Rick, she realized. She was in love with the man. She was certain of it. As certain as she was that she couldn't handle it, no matter how hard she tried.

Running.

That was the real thing Emma was *amazing* at.

"THIS IS A BAD IDEA, MAN," Stephen said over the cell line.

"Tell me about it." Rick stared through the starless night outside his windshield, at the golden light shining through Emma's front curtains.

She'd blown him off. All day. No word on her meetings with either Olivia Sanchez or her boss. Not a single of his messages had been returned. At five o'clock, Rick had finally given in and called Brad Griffin, only to be told that she'd left hours earlier, after calling Stephen for a ride.

"She was okay when we dropped her off," his friend reassured Rick.

"Yeah."

"If she wanted to talk to you, she'd have—"

"Yeah, she'd have called me like we planned, instead of dragging you into the middle of this."

"But you're still sitting outside her house…."

"Yeah."

"You've got it bad, man."

"So it would seem."

Maybe Rick hadn't felt much in a long time, just as Carter thought. But *not feeling* wasn't possible around Emma. She was unpredictable. Exciting as hell. Worth every crazy thing she made him feel. And impossible for Rick to walk away from, no matter how many times she shut him out.

Emma was someone Rick would always need more of, the same way his dad would always need Rick's mom. And after their kiss that morning, Rick had let himself believe that *more* was something Emma was finally letting herself want with him.

"Did Emma say anything about her interview with Sanchez?" he asked Stephen.

"Nope. Barely spoke to Randy or me at all. And let me just say, that's a tension-filled two hours of my life I'll never get back. Griffin wouldn't fill you in?"

"Nope."

But the interview obviously hadn't gone well.

"So, you're going to the source, then?"

"Yeah."

He'd barged through her door once before. He could do it again. He had to. He'd dragged her into this Sanchez mess, and he wasn't leaving her alone to deal with the fallout. Not to mention that *he* needed more. More of Emma's passion and her laughter and her trust—even if she was clearly outside her comfort zone with all of it. Who wasn't?

"Go with God," his friend said before hanging up.

Go for what *he* needed, had been Carter's advice—a man who couldn't let go of the one-and-only woman he'd ever loved.

And for the first time, Rick was finally starting to understand where his father was coming from.

CHAPTER FIFTEEN

RICK HAD EXPECTED Jessie to answer the bell.
He'd hoped that maybe making the kid laugh
again would be a safe way to ease into the
house. So when Emma opened up and stood
staring at him, looking beautiful and exhausted and as off balance as he felt, he
suddenly couldn't find his voice.

She hesitantly waved him in. Then she
shut the door and leaned against it.

She'd changed into fleecy sweats. Pink
ones. They were too big, like all her clothes
were now. But her petite frame wasn't dimin-
ished by them. She was clearly nervous.
Upset. But the strength that had first drawn
him to her was still there.

"I thought maybe you'd be resting," he
started. "I was expecting your daughter to be
standing guard."

"I'm eating some cereal, then I was
going to turn in. Jessie's..." Her hand

fussed with the hem of her sweatshirt. "She's off school tomorrow for a teacher workday, so she wanted to spend the night with a friend."

"You okay here alone?" he asked, before the ridiculousness of the question sank in. "I mean, of course you are. Stephen just told me how exhausted you were when he dropped you off. And you didn't call, so I figured maybe…"

"You figured maybe I needed my teenage daughter to take care of me?"

Care certainly wasn't what was flashing through Rick's mind as he fantasized about separating Emma from her sweats.

"Thanks to your source's information, the Sanchez case is going nowhere fast." She left him to follow or not, as she walked toward the kitchen.

Of course he followed.

The back of her, all covered in pink, was as distracting as the front.

"I wanted to talk with you about that. But the case isn't the only reason I'm here."

"Really?" Her cereal was only half-eaten. She dumped it into the sink, then busied herself rinsing the bowl and loading it into the open dishwasher. When she stepped to the coffeemaker to set up a pot, even though she'd told him she was getting ready for bed, it was the final straw.

"Damn it, Emma! Would you talk to me, please?"

She abandoned the coffee and turned toward him. Her expression was wary. But her gaze… Something in her eyes reached out to him.

"I couldn't stop thinking about you all day," he admitted. "I'd hoped you'd let me know how things went with Olivia. But I was hoping for more than that…."

"More?" She looked so damn scared.

"I needed to hear your voice again." He could see the courage fighting through her fear. "It was a long, frustrating day. And somewhere along the line, I realized I couldn't go to bed tonight without being near you again."

He stepped closer when all she did was stare.

"Do you want to talk about the case?"

She started to shake her head. Then she sighed instead.

"How credible is your source?" she asked.

"Very."

"So this Cisco Romero is definitely linked to Olivia Sanchez, and most likely where the drugs your guys found in her apartment came from?"

"That doesn't mean Olivia knew they were there." Rick wished he could sound more encouraging.

"Or maybe she did, and she's not the self-sacrificing mother we hoped she was?" There were tears in Emma's eyes. But she smiled that professional smile Rick had seen so many times. "If that's the case, those kids would be better off anywhere but in a home where their mother is dealing drugs and using them to help her do it."

"You warned me from the start that Olivia might really be guilty," he reminded her. "I gather things didn't go any better down at county than they did on Monday."

Emma sniffed, and blinked until her eyes cleared.

"There's no way Olivia Sanchez is simply a scared woman, protecting her family in a no-win situation. Not after what I saw today."

"And what was that?"

"Someone whose secrets are more important to her than her family."

"I'm sorry." He could feel Emma blaming herself. Thinking about her own mother.

"I mean, I can't make her put her kids first, right?" Emma stiffened as he tugged her toward him. "If she's covering for Romero, then—"

"Then that makes her an accessory at the very least. And you'll defend your guilty client as best you can, while you protect her kids. Whether she realizes it or not, Olivia is lucky to have you on her side."

"Right, because I've done such a bang-up job for her so far."

"Even if she has to plea out the way Brad and Jeff planned from the start, you're still her best shot at seeing daylight through something besides cinder blocks and barbed wire anytime soon. Her bad choices aren't your fault, Emma. If you want to blame somebody, blame me for—"

"You were making sure you did the right thing by a suspect," she argued. "No matter what it cost your career. I'm…grateful you thought I was what you needed. Really. I'll still do the best I can, but—"

"But there's no keeping this family together?"

She shook her head once. And that was that, the coolness in her gaze said. Time for Rick to leave her to deal with her demons alone.

Except he wasn't going anywhere.

"I lied," he said instead, slipping his

hands down her arms. "I'm not sorry, about any of this."

"Rick—"

"I know finishing this case is going to be hard." His hands found hers. "And I'm the one who talked you into getting involved when the odds were stacked against the Sanchez family from the start. But I'm not sorry for the last week, Emma. You're on your feet again. And you're in my arms. How can I be sorry about that?"

"Rick, don't…" She tried to tug away.

"Don't want what's happening between us? You really expect me to go back to being just another cop that you question in court every now and then, and let what's between us go?"

"You were never just another cop." She inched closer, but not close enough. "And I was wrong to ever think that you or your father were the enemy. You were doing your jobs, both of you, with the same passion and commitment I used to have for mine."

"Used to have? You dragged yourself downtown today, when you were barely able to crawl out of bed a week ago."

"So I could decide that the best thing for a family was to rip a mother away from her kids!"

"And you think that makes you a bad public defender?"

"I ran from county, Rick. Again. I should have headed for the D.A.'s office, then to lunch with Jeff. Worked out whatever plea deal I could. But instead, I ran. You think I'm the fighter I used to be. The lawyer you knew and the woman who raised her brothers. But it's too much. Since the shooting…all I know how to do anymore is run."

"No, you've been recovering, and you're not completely there yet. You'll deal with Olivia tomorrow, because that's who you are. But for tonight, maybe the best thing to do *is* to let it go?"

Emma stared up at him instead of answering.

"Fighting to get on with it all the time…" he said. "Take my word for it, it's not the answer I've thought it was."

He'd fought to protect the public. To help his dad. To help Emma. He'd done everything but face what he really wanted—what he was too afraid to reach for.

"You'll do everything you can for the Sanchez family," he said. "Tomorrow. But tonight, how about letting it go and focusing on something else? I came here because I couldn't stop thinking about us."

"Us?" She sounded more afraid than shocked. "If… If this is about you feeling obligated—"

"Obligation? Is that what you think this morning was? Or last night? When we're together, I'm usually feeling a powerful urge to shake you. Or kiss you. Or both. But I wouldn't exactly call what I'm feeling obligation."

"I… I can't do this. I can't keep doing this… Whatever we're doing."

"Love?" he pushed himself to say. "Is that what we're doing?"

Her hand turned in his, finally holding on instead of pulling away. He didn't move a muscle. He didn't dare.

"We're…" Her thumb rubbed the inside of his wrist. "I'm not…"

"Yes, we are." His fingers stroked the top of her hand. Carefully. Slowly. The catch in her breath spiked his heart rate, drawing him closer. "And yes, we can, if we can both stop fighting this long enough to actually feel it at the same time. No excuses. No legal distractions. No family interruptions. Just us, and what we need. Just tonight."

She shook her head. She was shaking all over. And that's when Rick knew he had her. Because he was shaking, too. And they were both still holding on.

"I can't…" she began. "At the interview today, when I realized what I was going to have to do, I started thinking about my mother again. I…I thought of you. I needed you there, to keep the past from closing in…."

And then she'd run.

He pulled her to his chest, tucking her head under his chin, and rubbed a soothing hand along her delicate spine. He smiled as he felt her relax against him.

"I need you, too, Emma. I have, ever since that night in your office. So much my world's going to implode if you leave me in this alone. I've blamed my father for years, for falling apart after my mother's death. But now I get what Carter's been going through. It's making me crazy, not being able to be near you for just one damn day."

Emma tensed at his admission, but by the time he tilted her chin up, fire was flashing in her eyes. Her body arched, bringing her mouth closer. He kissed her harder than he'd planned to. But she was there with him, kissing him back, her sweet desperation making him crave more.

"You're good for me, Monty," he said.

Tiny wrinkles marred her forehead. "Why?"

"Why don't we figure that out tonight, together? Just us, being good for each other. Forget that this scares the shit out of both of us. Don't run anymore, Emma. Let go, and be with me."

"I…" Her eyes filled with the determination he'd fallen for the first time he'd faced her in court, and the vulnerability that broke his heart every time she let him see it. "I'm not sure I can."

"If there's one thing I know for certain, it's that you can do anything you set your mind to."

Emma blinked. Then she gave him an impish grin that was the sexiest thing he'd ever seen.

"You said something like that the first day you came here."

"I…I…" He was the one stammering now. Her fingers had lifted to the zipper of her sweatshirt. "What?"

"You basically told me that the woman you knew before the shooting never would have allowed herself to become the weakling I was."

"I never thought you were weak."

"No, you haven't." The soft whoosh of the zipper lowering, the glimpse of flesh that lay bare beneath, flashed fire through Rick. "I think that's why it's impossible for me to feel weak when you're around."

"What?" The buzzing in his ears drowned out what she was saying.

She let the two halves of the sweatshirt fall free, revealing creamy skin and the edge of the scar marring her tiny waist.

"Would you like a tour of the rest of the house?" she asked.

And that was when what she was saying, instead of the way her body was torturing him, finally had his full attention. Her expression remained a flirty challenge, but her voice wasn't steady. She wasn't sure. She wasn't in control. But she was letting go anyway.

"Lead the way." He dropped a hand to her waist, determined to make the risk pay off for both of them.

LEAD THE WAY....

Emma walked ahead of Rick, into the dimness of her bedroom. She wasn't going to stop this. How could she, when her entire body felt alive again?

But the shadows were still there, all around them. Reminding her of the past, and what feeling this much could cost if it all fell apart again.

"I think we need to be clear about our expectations," she warned.

Rick's gaze slid down her breasts to her waist, to the exaggerated curve that pregnancy had made out of her hips. Each step he took toward her was predatory. Possessive. His body tensed as he stopped less than an inch away. He reached a hand to the drawstrings of her sweats, then pulled.

"I'm feeling pretty clear about things. How 'bout you?"

In Emma's experience, smiles could be evil. They could be manipulative. Or they could transform your world, when you found the kind of smile you'd give anything to keep. Rick's mouth curled up at the corners with the brand of heat that could convince even a cynical woman that she'd never need anything else to be happy.

"I'm not *a trust your feelings and everything will be fine* kind of girl, Lieutenant. I've never had the luxury of indulging in dreams like that." Dreams she'd never wanted as badly as she wanted what he was promising.

"So it's wham, bam, thank you, ma'am, that you're looking for?" Testing his theory, Rick roamed a hand inside her loosened waistband, tracking her reaction closely.

He caught every pound of her pulse at the base of her neck. He watched her breasts rise and fall with every breath. His pupils dilated at the exact moment she felt her nipples tighten painfully.

"I want you," she admitted. "But I just can't… anything else. It's… If you're going to—"

"Shhh…" His thumb rubbed across her bottom lip. "Relax. No expectations. No anything else. Just tonight. Just now. We can figure the rest out tomorrow. Trust me, Emma. I'd never hurt you."

His other hand closed around the arms she hadn't realized she'd crossed over her chest, and gently pulled them away. He cupped the underside of her breast, shaping it, his thumb rasping over the tip like sandpaper on velvet. An answering zing of need shot downward to her toes, then back up again.

"Let yourself feel, Monty," he challenged. "Let this be good…."

"It…" It *was* good. Too good. "I want…"

"Yes?" He skimmed her sweats down her

thighs, groaning at the magenta thong she hadn't taken off when she changed out of her suit. "It's a constant distraction, what kind of naughty you had going on under your clothes, Counselor. As always, you don't disappoint."

And neither did he.

His strong hands made fast work of her underwear. Then, before she could rouse herself to step completely out of her clothes, he'd lifted her until their eyes were level, their bodies perfectly aligned. His muscles didn't even strain as he kept her suspended. Then his palms settled beneath her bottom, and he walked the few steps to the bed. He lowered her to her satin spread, his body never breaking contact with hers.

His, fully clothed.

Hers, completely vulnerable. Open. But safe, just as he'd promised.

"Do you trust me?" he asked.

She nodded so slowly, it might have been a dream. It must have been a dream. Because, heaven help her, she did trust him. She dragged her hands down muscle after muscle, to where his T-shirt was tucked into his jeans. She gave herself up to the shadows and the night.

She let the fear go.

And she prayed that, come morning, she'd

be strong enough to keep trusting Rick—and to trust herself enough to do what she had to do next, for both of them.

CHAPTER SIXTEEN

CARTER PULLED INTO the driveway. His son's truck was back in its normal spot at the curb—where it hadn't been first thing that morning. He parked in the garage, killed the ignition, and let the car sounds rattle to a halt. Finally, the world was silent around him.

Pulling the list the doctor had given him from his shirt pocket, he scanned the damn thing. Then he let his attention stray to the sky-blue Beetle collecting dust on the other side of the two-car garage. Melissa's baby. She'd be pissed if she could see it now.

Standing out back yesterday, after he'd gotten home from lunch with Rick, looking at Melissa's garden and thinking about which green thing he'd kill next, contemplating the drink in his hand, Carter had finally gotten it. What five years of holding on to his grief had cost him.

They were living together, he and his boy, so neither one of them was alone. And thank God for that, because Carter probably would have put a gun to his head years ago if Rick hadn't hung around pestering his ass. But they weren't really living. Neither of them.

So Carter had made a call late last night to a doctor friend. And he'd gotten into his car that morning, hangover and all, and made the trip to get the ball rolling. Now, he was home to do only one thing before packing and heading out again—leave his boy a message that he was too much of a coward to say in person.

At least he would, after he took one last look at the garden he was going to call a lawn service to level and replant with permanent shrubs and trees. He was contacting a car dealer, too, to come by next week and cart the dead Beetle away.

Carter hauled himself to his feet and ran his fingers across the baby-blue paint and dust covering Melissa's car. Then he headed toward the backyard, ready to say a goodbye that he'd been putting off saying for far too long.

RICK DUG ANOTHER rotting plant from the flower bed he'd been demolishing for the last half hour. With a flip of his shovel, he tossed the carcass of what had once been a dwarf nandina onto a pile of its skeletal friends.

And onto a familiar-looking boot.

"What the hell are you doing!" his father thundered, as if Rick were desecrating the man's gloomy shrine.

Rick had found Carter gone when he got home that morning, and it had seemed like an open invitation to indulge in his old man's favorite pastime. So had the fact that Emma hadn't been lying next to Rick when he'd woken in her bed.

Do you trust me?

Guess Rick had his answer.

"Where you been, Dad?" He trenched the shovel under another dead shrub.

"Get the hell away from Melissa's garden!" Carter responded, sounding downright sober.

"No." Rick popped the bush free and tossed it his dad's way. Carter sidestepped, then grabbed the shovel out of Rick's hands.

"What the hell are you doin!" the man repeated.

Rick was feeling, damn it! Wasn't it obvious? Wasn't the garden the official place for the Downing men to lose their minds over women they couldn't keep?

He yanked the shovel back.

"So, did you boink the public defender last night?" Carter ranted. "Is that it?"

The shovel hit the ground. Rick's hands hit his hips in an attempt not to haul his father up by his dress shirt.

Dress shirt?

Rick checked his watch. "It's not even noon. Where have you been?"

Carter's bluster disappeared so quickly, Rick reached for him.

"Are you okay?" he asked.

"Get yourself cleaned up and come inside, and we'll talk about it."

"I don't think so." Inside where the booze was. "We can talk about it right here. Where were you when I got home this morning?"

"Where were you when I woke up?" Carter shook his head when Rick didn't answer. "I'm assuming things didn't turn out any better than I warned you they would, since you're here and Emma Montgomery's...where exactly?"

"I have no idea." Rick put the shovel back to good use.

Emma had been fire in his arms last night. A living heat he'd woken wanting all over again. Now it felt as if his heart was trying to pump ice through his veins.

"You're an idiot," his father spat at him. "Why are you letting the woman go, if you're so hung up on her?"

"I'm doing what she clearly wants. What you told me to do. I'm leaving her the hell alone."

"You're picking *now* to care what I think about anything? To quit?"

"I'm not—"

"You're hopeless about the woman. You clearly got into something with her last night, besides talking about that damn case. But—"

"The case is done. I clued Barrette in this morning on my source's latest information. We'll know more after a DEA sting on Friday, but it looks like Olivia Sanchez really is mixed up with the drugs we found, all the way up to her eyeballs."

"Well, that had to have made Barrette's day. Jeff Caldwell's, too."

"Yeah, the captain didn't even blink when I told him I needed someone to cover my shift today. Said I'd earned it."

"Cover? Why? So you can kill my garden and celebrate being an idiot, just like your old man?"

Rick stomped toward the rusted-out

wheelbarrow, dragged it back and began to load up the dead plants.

Flashes of Emma—lost in making love, lost in him, open and free and needing and trusting him to share it all—roared back.

"If Emma Montgomery's so important to you, why aren't you with her, convincing her?"

"She was gone this morning, when I woke up." She hadn't trusted him enough to face the day together. To face the difficulties, and the possibilities, of the future they could have. "If I thought she… If I thought it would do any good, I'd… She's just gone, okay!"

"I don't know." Carter looked down at the dead bushes, then at Rick. "Is it?"

Rick looked, too. At the dreary, overcast day. At the mess he was making. Then back to the man who was actually standing there, focused on Rick's pain instead of his own. Bossing him around like any other father would.

"Of course it's not okay that she's gone." They weren't talking about just Emma now. But they *were* talking, there in Rick's mother's favorite place. Both upset. Both sober. "It hurts like a son of a bitch."

Carter nodded. He pulled a folded piece of paper from his pocket and opened it. "Well, then I guess you should do something about that, while you still have the chance." He handed the single sheet over.

North View Hospital: Detoxification Clinic Admissions Checklist, read the heading at the top of the page. While Rick was still trying to process the reality of what he was looking at, his father handed over a business card.

"Al-Anon?" Rick stopped gaping at the small rectangle of paper in time to catch his father silently walking toward the house.

"Dad?" He headed after him, tripped on the rake he'd been using before the shovel and barely kept himself from taking a header in the scum-riddled goldfish pond.

"They tell me I'll be out in two weeks." Carter stopped and turned toward him. In the shade of his wife's favorite magnolia tree, his shaggy hair brushed and his clothes neat and maybe even clean, Carter looked like a reflection of the man Rick had idolized throughout his childhood. "When I get home, don't let me catch you out here, still digging in this godforsaken place."

He gazed around his wife's sanctuary.

"This is no life for either one of us, Ricky. I dragged you into it with me, I know. And you stuck it out. But you're hiding here, same as me. Me and the job are what *you* do to hide. What you fight for, instead of what you need. And that ain't right. You can't let that be all there is."

"God, Dad."

Rick hadn't wanted to hope this was possible. And now it was happening. His dad was leaving, so he could start pulling his life together.

"Do…" His voice flamed out on the first try. "Do you want me to drive you over?"

"No. I'm doing this myself. You've babysat me enough, son." Carter shook his head. "You go figure a way out of your own mess. You deserve better than this, Rick. And I'm thinking, so does that sexy public defender of yours. The woman's definitely growing on me. She's got to be something special if she's got you spinning this badly."

EMMA HAD WORKED since early that morning to make sure everything was solid. Ever since she'd called Jessie at Caroline's to be sure her daughter was okay hanging there most of the day. Ever since she'd left Rick without an explanation.

Only now she couldn't move.

"You want me to run the options past

her?" Brad asked outside the interview room where Olivia Sanchez was waiting for them. "You've done all the work with the D.A. It's pretty straightforward from here, and I don't mind—"

"No, it's not straightforward." Emma reached for the door. "Not for me."

"I got nothing to say to either of you," their defendant insisted as they stepped inside. "I want a guard to take me to my cell."

"Not until you listen up." Emma forced a neutral expression as she sat across the table from Olivia. "Because none of us is leaving here until you agree to one of the D.A.'s offers."

"I ain't got to agree to nothin'."

"One is the same deal we discussed with the district attorney already," Brad said as he opened the file he'd removed from his brief-case. "You plead guilty. The case goes to a directed verdict from the judge, then to sentencing. Quick and easy, and you're off the front page of the newspaper by Monday."

"Except—" Emma watched closely, still needing to be wrong about the woman. "The offer's ten years now, not five."

"What!"

"Recent developments the APD has just brought to light suggest strongly that you are, in fact, guilty," Emma continued. "There's every indication that the new information will be confirmed, which disinclines the D.A. to continue to deal down the sentence in your favor."

"Disin—what?" Real fear crept into the other woman's eyes. "What new information?"

"Confirmation of your ongoing relationship with Cisco Romero. Which leads me to the D.A.'s second offer, one I strongly suggest you consider."

Emma waited for Olivia to make eye contact. Then she waited some more.

"What second offer?" the other woman finally asked. She slapped her hand to the table. "The cops have the drugs. I'm going down. What else is there?"

Brad inched his chair closer to Emma, better buffering her from Olivia. "Ms. Montgomery's worked out a get-out-of-jail-free card for you. I think you should listen up."

"Card? What card?"

"Cisco Romero," Emma said, reclaiming her voice. She nodded her thanks to Brad for his support. "You roll on him, give the federal authorities whatever they want—whatever you know about his operations—

and you and your boys will be relocated and protected with new identities."

"Just like that."

"Just like that," Emma answered. "Of course, you'll be closely monitored to make sure you never again go near narcotics or subject your children to the dangerous lifestyle you've dragged them into here. That part of your life will be over. But you'll get a second chance at being a mother. You and your boys will stay together.

"You…you don't know what you're asking me to do."

Actually, Emma did, and that's what made the emptiness in the other woman's stare so difficult to stomach. Because no matter how hard Emma had fought to get the D.A. to secure the protective custody deal from the feds—a second chance that *her* mother never had—Emma couldn't make Olivia take it and save her family.

"It's simple. All you have to do is decide what's most important to you. A new future with your boys? Or your lover and the drug life that got you into this situation."

Just like Emma had to decide between grabbing hold of the man whose love offered her a new, risky future, or clinging to the life of running that was all she'd really known for years.

"YEAH, I'M HERE." Rick said into his cell while he paced the county jail's central waiting area. "I haven't seen Emma or Brad Griffin yet. But they both logged in forty-five minutes ago."

"Don't make me regret not meeting you down there, man," Stephen warned. "If I wasn't due in court in fifteen, I'd—"

"Well, you are. So let me go find our girl, and I'll leave you a voice mail once I know something."

"I know she's driving you crazy, Rick. But cut her some slack. If you care about her—"

"Care about her? I love the woman!" Rick shouted in frustration.

He realized what he'd said. Everyone milling around the waiting area had heard him loud and clear, too.

"Not that that's doing me a lot of good," he said more calmly into the phone. "Since I can't seem to keep my hands on her. Why the hell would she come down here again on her own? I thought she'd…" Never mind what he'd thought. "You still have no idea what she's meeting with Sanchez about?"

"Nope," his friend said. "I told you all I know. The buzz is she's getting the plea done today. And it's sounding like it's big. After tomorrow's arraignment, she should be able to put the case behind her."

The case, and maybe the cop who'd gotten her into it, too.

Rick slapped his phone closed and kept pacing. Kept telling himself that Emma running from him to take care of the Sanchez case was better than her simply running. Except the case was clearly still tearing her apart, and whatever she'd felt she had to do about it, she'd thought she had to do alone.

Once Stephen had finally returned his three messages that morning, to relay Emma's whereabouts, Rick hadn't even taken the time to clean up from working in the garden. He'd headed into town, dirt-covered jeans and all, to confront Emma. To fight for her.

I need to do the right thing for the Sanchez case, she'd supposedly told Randy, when she'd called him for a ride while Rick still slept.

And she hadn't wanted Rick there while she did it.

He got it. He understood how hard

trusting was. But he was tired of being shut out by the people he loved, because they couldn't handle—

His cell's ring made him look at the display, expecting another call from Stephen. Not recognizing the number, he pocketed the thing. When he looked up, Emma was pushing through the doors leading away from the interview rooms, her phone to her ear.

She hung up when she saw him, and his cell quieted. She stopped, Brad Griffin at her side.

"Lieutenant Downing." The attorney held out his hand to shake.

Emma didn't say anything.

Rick didn't move a muscle.

"I woke up alone this morning," he said, his gaze locked with Emma's. "In *your* house. Your bed. You wanna tell me exactly why that was necessary?"

"Well." Griffin's arm dropped to his side. He glanced nervously between his boss and Rick. "It looks as if you have another ride, Emma. Good work in there. I guess I'll see you at the courthouse."

The man couldn't have gotten out of there faster if he'd sprinted for the front door.

Emma held up the slip of paper he'd given

her yesterday. "I tried to call you just now, after we finished up."

It wasn't exactly an answer to Rick's question, but it was a promising start.

"Finishing up what?" he asked.

"Facing what I was letting my past do to this case." Her eyes were damp, but her beautiful voice was crystal clear. "What I was letting it do to my life. I had to take care of that, Rick."

"Alone?" He'd asked for just one more night. Was that really all he was going to get? "I thought we… I thought you'd at least learned you could trust me with this case."

"I do trust you."

She slipped her phone into her briefcase and motioned him to a pair of nearby chairs, giving them a speck of privacy in the crowded room.

"You're the reason I was strong enough to do this. Any of it. If it wasn't for you, I'd still be sleeping the day away, drowning in memories."

"And if it wasn't for you," Rick said, "my dad wouldn't have gotten riled up enough to give a damn about what I'm doing, or whether or not he wants to be any part of my life anymore. Or his own, for that matter." Rick had to let her know what she'd meant to his life already, even if she was never ready to mean more. "Thanks to you barging in and making me love you, my dad's on his way to detox right now. That's how good you've been for me. And that's what makes your leaving so—"

"Wait a minute. You love me?" Her hand felt blindly for his, while their gazes stayed glued to one another.

"I…" Rick hung his head and stared at their joined hands. "I love you, Monty. And whether you can handle it or not, I'm going to keep loving you for the rest of my life."

"I…" She was clinging to him now, as if her life depended on him not letting go. "I…I fought for a plea deal I knew Olivia Sanchez wouldn't take. I threw my weight around with D.A. Lewis and likely turned Jeff's hair white, but I got her the chance for Federal relocation and protection if she rolled on Romero. It would have made you smell even more like roses with the DEA and your Chief."

"That's… That's great. But…" He didn't give a damn about his career right now. "What do you mean, Olivia wouldn't take it?"

"I gave her a choice to have a new life. It was the perfect deal." Emma sounded close to tears, but her eyes were clear. "But she'd rather give up her kids than roll on Cisco."

Rick wasn't certain he'd heard her right. "What?"

"She couldn't let go of what she knew, no…no matter what it cost her to keep it. She chose prison—ten years of it—instead of protective custody with her family. At least those boys will be safe now, without her. At least… It's the best thing for them. Really, if she cares that little about them…"

"Emma." Rick fought to take it all in. To understand. To imagine how hard the last few hours must have been for her. But she'd done what she had to. No matter her own memories. No more running. "You did all you could. I doubt any other lawyer in town could have negotiated protective relocation. Now you know for sure that Olivia was a threat to her family. You've given her boys a clean start. Probably saved their lives."

Emma nodded. Wiped at her eyes. Then she gave him a sad smile he'd have given anything to make brighter.

"Why didn't you let me be here to help you?" he asked, letting himself hope, the way loving her had taught him to.

He'd come determined to fight for her, for

what he needed. Instead he waited, knowing this victory was a moment Emma had struggled fifteen years to reach.

"Because—" her smiled widened "—I love you, too, Rick, and I had to be sure. The past— I had to be sure it wouldn't be between us. That I could let it go, and give you back everything you give me every time you butt into my life because you can't help yourself. Every time you reach for me, like you'll never let go."

"I won't let go. Ever." Rick smiled in return, his mind recording every detail of the moment when he'd finally found a lifelong love of his own.

"Neither will I," she promised, freedom in her voice and her smile. Freedom from the shadows.

"What I don't get," he said, looking forward to the years ahead, filled with her love and her courage and everything Emma did to keep him on his toes, "is what you were so worried about. I've already told you, Monty. There's absolutely nothing you can't do, even learning how to trust a no-good cop like me."

"Trust *and* love, Lieutenant." She leaned forward, her smile becoming a searing kiss. "I want them both with you, and I want an ironclad, unbreakable arrangement."

"You've got yourself a deal, Counselor." Rick returned her kiss, absorbing the reality that he'd have Emma in his arms, in his heart, every day for the rest of their lives. "You've got yourself a deal."

* * * * *

Turn the page for a sneak preview of
AFTERSHOCK,
a new anthology featuring New York Times
bestselling author Sharon Sala.

Available October 2008.

n●cturne ™

Dramatic and sensual tales of
paranormal romance.

Chapter 1

October
New York City

Nicole Masters was sitting cross-legged on her sofa while a cold autumn rain peppered the windows of her fourth-floor apartment. She was poking at the ice cream in her bowl and trying not to be in a mood.

Six weeks ago, a simple trip to her neighborhood pharmacy had turned into a nightmare. She'd walked into the middle of a robbery. She never even saw the man who shot her in the head and left her for dead. She'd survived, but some of her senses had not. She was dealing with short-term memory loss and a tendency to stagger. Even though she'd been told the problems were most likely temporary, she waged a daily battle with depression.

Her parents had been killed in a car wreck

when she was twenty-one. And except for a few friends—and most recently her boyfriend, Dominic Tucci, who lived in the apartment right above hers, she was alone. Her doctor kept reminding her that she should be grateful to be alive, and on one level she knew he was right. But he wasn't living in her shoes.

If she'd been anywhere else but at that pharmacy when the robbery happened, she wouldn't have died twice on the way to the hospital. Instead of being grateful that she'd survived, she couldn't stop thinking of what she'd lost.

But that wasn't the end of her troubles. On top of everything else, something strange was happening inside her head. She'd begun to hear odd things: sounds, not voices—at least, she didn't think they were voices. It was more like the distant noise of rapids—a rush of wind and water inside her head that, when it came, blocked out everything around her. It didn't happen often, but when it did, it was frightening, and it was driving her crazy.

The blank moments, which is what she called them, even had a rhythm. First there came that sound, then a cold sweat, then panic with no reason. Part of her feared it was the beginning of an emotional breakdown. And part of her feared it wasn't—that it was going to turn out to be a permanent souvenir of her resurrection.

Frustrated with herself and the situation as it stood, she upped the sound on the TV remote. But instead of *Wheel of Fortune,* an announcer broke in with a special bulletin.

"This just in. Police are on the scene of a kidnapping that occurred only hours ago at The Dakota. Molly Dane, the six-year-old daughter of one of Holly-wood's blockbuster stars, Lyla Dane, was taken by force from the family apartment. At this time they have yet to receive a ransom demand. The house-keeper was seriously injured during the abduction, and is, at the present time, in surgery. Police are hoping to be able to talk to her once she regains conscious-ness. In the meantime, we are going now to a press conference with Lyla Dane."

Horrified, Nicole stilled as the cameras went live to where the actress was speaking before a bank of microphones. The shock and terror in Lyla Dane's voice were physically painful to watch. But even though Nicole kept upping the volume, the sound continued to fade.

Just when she was beginning to think something was wrong with her set, the broadcast suddenly switched from the Dane press conference to what appeared to be footage of the kidnapping, beginning with footage from inside the apartment.

When the front door suddenly flew back against the wall and four men rushed in, Nicole gasped. Horrified, she quickly realized that this must have been caught on a security camera inside the Dane apartment.

As Nicole continued to watch, a small Asian woman, who she guessed was the maid, rushed forward in an effort to keep them out. When one of the men hit her in the face with his gun, Nicole moaned. The violence was too reminiscent of what she'd lived through. Sick to her stomach, she fisted her hands against her belly, wishing it was over, but unable to tear her gaze away.

When the maid dropped to the carpet, the same man followed with a vicious kick to the little woman's midsection that lifted her off the floor.

"Oh, my God," Nicole said. When blood

began to pool beneath the maid's head, she started to cry.

As the tape played on, the four men split up in different directions. The camera caught one running down a long marble hallway, then disappearing into a room. Moments later he reappeared, carrying a little girl, who Nicole assumed was Molly Dane. The child was wearing a pair of red pants and a white turtleneck sweater, and her hair was partially blocking her abductor's face as he carried her down the hall. She was kicking and screaming in his arms, and when he slapped her, it elicited an agonized scream that brought the other three running. Nicole watched in horror as one of them ran up and put his hand over Molly's face. Seconds later, she went limp.

One moment they were in the foyer, then they were gone.

Nicole jumped to her feet, then staggered drunkenly. The bowl of ice cream she'd absentmindedly placed in her lap shattered at her feet, splattering glass and melting ice cream everywhere.

The picture on the screen abruptly switched from the kidnapping to what Nicole assumed was a rerun of Lyla Dane's plea for her daughter's safe return, but she was numb.

Before she could think what to do next, the doorbell rang. Startled by the unexpected sound, she shakily swiped at the tears and took a step forward. She didn't feel the glass shards piercing her feet until she took the second step. At that point, sharp pains shot through her foot. She gasped, then looked down in confusion. Her legs looked as if she'd been running through mud, and she was standing in broken glass and ice cream, while a thin ribbon of blood seeped out from beneath her toes.

"Oh, no," Nicole mumbled, then stifled a second moan of pain.

The doorbell rang again. She shivered, then clutched her head in confusion.

"Just a minute!" she yelled, then tried to sidestep the rest of the debris as she hobbled to the door.

When she looked through the peephole in the door, she didn't know whether to be relieved or regretful.

It was Dominic, and as usual, she was a mess.

Nicole smiled a little self-consciously as she opened the door to let him in. "I just don't know what's happening to me. I think I'm losing my mind."

"Hey, don't talk about my woman like that."

Nicole rode the surge of delight his words brought. "So I'm still your woman?"

Dominic lowered his head.

Their lips met.

The kiss proceeded.

Slowly.

Thoroughly.

* * * * *

Be sure to look for the
AFTERSHOCK
*anthology next month, as well as other
exciting paranormal stories
from Silhouette Nocturne.
Available in October
wherever books are sold.*

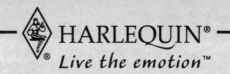

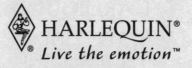

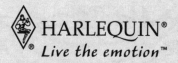

Harlequin® Historical
Historical Romantic Adventure!

Imagine a time of chivalrous knights and unconventional ladies, roguish rakes and impetuous heiresses, rugged cowboys and spirited frontierswomen— these rich and vivid tales will capture your imagination!

Harlequin Historical . . . they're too good to miss!

HARLEQUIN®
Presents

The world's bestselling romance series...
The series that brings you your favorite authors,
month after month:

Helen Bianchin...Emma Darcy
Lynne Graham...Penny Jordan
Miranda Lee...Sandra Marton
Anne Mather...Carole Mortimer
Melanie Milburne...Michelle Reid

and many more talented authors!

Wealthy, powerful, gorgeous men...
Women who have feelings just like your own...
The stories you love, set in exotic, glamorous locations...

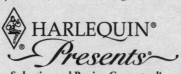

HARLEQUIN®
Presents

Seduction and Passion Guaranteed!

HPDIR08

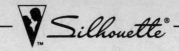

SPECIAL EDITION™

Emotional, compelling stories that capture the intensity of living, loving and creating a family in today's world.

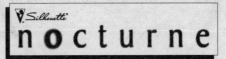

Modern, passionate reads that are powerful and provocative.

nocturne

Dramatic and sensual tales of paranormal romance.

Romances that are sparked by danger and fueled by passion.